Had the previous night really been a mistake?

Lucinda feared that it had and Diego's words confirmed it.

"Last night proved to me," he said, "that for us to live at Pobla de Cabres, in the same house, must not happen. I can't rely on myself not to make another pass at you. I know you didn't intend to be provocative, but you obviously don't understand that I have a low boiling point. To put it bluntly, it's been a long time since I have made love...and you are a very lovely girl."

He paused, then added, "I won't apologize for what happened, but I can't allow it to happen again."

"Are you saying it would have happened with any girl within arm's reach?" Lucinda asked quietly, knowing that if he said yes, it would break her heart.

ANNE WEALE and her husband live in a Spanish villa high above the Mediterranean. An active woman, Anne enjoys swimming, interior decorating and antique hunting. But most of all she loves traveling. Researching new romantic backgrounds, she has explored New England, Florida, Canada, Australia, Italy, the Caribbean and the Pacific.

ANNE WEALE

catalan christmas

Harlequin Books

TORONTO • NEW YORK • LONDON
AMSTERDAM • PARIS • SYDNEY • HAMBURG
STOCKHOLM • ATHENS • TOKYO • MILAN

Harlequin Presents first edition December 1988
ISBN 0-373-11133-9

Original hardcover edition published in 1988
by Mills & Boon Limited

CHAPTER ONE

PARKED outside the butcher's shop in the *plaza* at the centre of the village, the bronze BMW convertible, with its roof down, was an incongruous sight. As out of place as old Miguel's horse-drawn cart would have been on the fast *autopista* which snaked down the east coast of Spain from the mountainous frontier in the north to the popular package-tour resorts on the Costa Blanca.

Arriving in the *plaza* on her bicycle, Lucinda noticed the car and its British registration at once, and wondered what tourists were doing in Sant Blai at this time of year.

The days were still warm and the slender, long-legged English girl was wearing shorts and a T-shirt. But the local people were dressed, as befitted the date on the calendar, in sweaters and cardigans. The season was over. The holiday apartments by the beach on the seaward edge of the *ribera*, as the delta was known to its inhabitants, had been shuttered and locked up for weeks past. It would be next summer before any foreigners, other than Lucinda herself, would be seen in the isolated village which owed its existence to the surrounding rice fields. Or so she would have thought before seeing the GB plate on the back of the sleek expensive car.

The doorway of Angelita's bakery still had its metallic fly curtain in place. Sweeping the strands aside with a practised movement of her bare brown forearm, Lucinda entered the shop and murmured the customary polite greeting to those who had arrived before her.

They were an old woman in black, the top of whose head barely reached Lucinda's shoulder; a stout matron wearing an apron and carrying a cotton bag containing several long loaves of bread from the nearby *panadería*; and a tall, good-looking man who was talking to Angelita.

Never having seen him before, Lucinda might have concluded he was the owner of the car, except that he was speaking in Catalan. A few of the foreigners who came to Sant Blai for summer holidays spoke some *castellano*, the principal language of Spain. None attempted to master the staccato Catalan which the locals spoke among themselves. Besides, studied more closely, he didn't look British. His hair was the color of old bronze, his skin olive. When he glanced, without interest, at her, she saw that his eyes had the tawny brilliance of a glass of sherry in sunlight. Casually well dressed, he had the look of someone from Barcelona, the capital of Catalonia and—according to the Catalans—the most dynamic, go-ahead city in Spain.

From behind the glassed-in display of pork chops, yellow-skinned chickens and mountain-bred lamb, Angelita was telling the stranger that somewhere was a difficult place to find.

Like many butchers' shops in Spain, this one was run by a woman who wielded her sharp knives and choppers with practised expertise, having learnt her trade from her mother. When Lucinda had first come to the delta to look after her grandfather and help him finish his book on the wild life of the region, it had driven her mad with impatience to have to wait her turn, sometimes for as long as half an hour, while the butcher and her customers chatted and Angelita cut and trimmed pieces of meat sufficient for only one meal. Planned, time-saving shopping seemed to be unknown in Spain, or at any rate in this backwater.

Gradually Lucinda had adapted to the leisurely pace of living until now she sometimes wondered if she would be able to re-adapt to the rush and bustle of London.

'This *senyor* is asking for the house of the English,' said Angelita, still speaking in Catalan and glancing at Lucinda as if merely to include her in the subject under discussion. Turning back to the man, she continued, 'Perhaps you haven't heard, *senyor*...the old Englishman has died. If your business is with him, you could have saved yourself a journey.'

'My business is with Senyorita Radstone.'

'Perhaps you should write a letter to her. It's only a few days since the funeral. She may not wish to see anyone who isn't a friend of the family,' said the butcher, with a glance Lucinda interpreted as a message that she need not reveal her identity if she didn't wish to.

'My business is urgent,' he said. 'If you'll give me directions, *senyora*, I expect I'll be able to find the house.'

Curious to know what he could want with her, and rather liking the look of him, Lucinda stepped forward and said, 'I can take you there, *senyor*...if you don't mind waiting until I've finished my shopping.'

For the first time he looked at her with attention. She guessed that, like most people seeing her in this environment, he took her for younger than she was. With her brown hair plaited into a single thick braid from the crown of her head to the centre of her shoulder-blades, and only a sun-screen lotion on her tanned and lightly freckled face, she could easily pass for eighteen.

In fact she was twenty-two and, dressed up, could look quite sophisticated. But here, in a basically peasant community where many older people could neither read nor write and a woman's place was still in the home, make-up and fashionable clothes seemed out of place except on Sundays and *fiestas*.

'Will that take long, *senyorita*?' the man asked.

She responded with the Spanish shrug which meant: Who can say... is it really important? 'You could have a coffee at the bar across the road while you're waiting,' she suggested.

He frowned and glanced at his watch, causing her to notice the beautiful shape of his hands.

'I haven't much time to spare,' he said. 'Could you, perhaps, do your shopping later? I have an appointment in Ulldecona at noon.'

'Then perhaps instead of going to the Englishman's *casita*, it would be more convenient to speak to the *senyorita* here in the village,' Lucinda suggested, still mystified by his business with her.

His expression lightened. 'Is that possible? You've seen her in Sant Blai?'

'She is here. You can talk in the bar. It won't be too noisy at this hour.'

There were certain times of day when the presence of a dozen or more men, all speaking loud Catalan, made any quiet conversation in the Bar Blau an impossibility.

The silvery strands of the fly-curtain were still swaying slightly from her entrance. Now Lucinda thrust them aside again and led the way out of the shop.

'Does the Englishwoman spend much time in the bar?' the man enquired, as they paused at the edge of the pavement before crossing the road which happened at that moment to be carrying more traffic than usual: a tractor going one way, a girl on a moped the other.

'Are you asking me if she drinks?' asked Lucinda, with a twinkle in her greeny-gray eyes.

'You know more about her than I do. I had never heard of her until a few days ago.' His sudden smile, replacing the look of barely-suppressed exasperation with the long-winded exchanges in the shop, was unexpectedly charming and persuasive. 'Does she?'

She shook her head. 'But she drinks wine as an *aperitivo*, which makes the old people stare.'

Visiting bars with her grandfather on their drives around the delta and sometimes in the mountainous hinterland, Lucinda had soon discovered that if Constantine Radstone ordered beer and she wanted a glass of wine, the beer would be placed before her. Spanish women of the rustic class drank wine only with their meals, and then sparingly.

'That's not unusual among the English,' he answered, taking her lightly by the elbow before they stepped into the road.

Such chivalrous gestures were not the norm in Sant Blai, but overt curiosity was.

'What is your name, *senyor*, and where are you from?' she enquired.

'Diego Montfalcó . . . from Barcelona.'

'But your car is marked Gran Bretaña?'

'I live and work in Londres. And you live near the house of these people from England, I gather? Do you know them well?'

'I knew the old man very well.' It amused her to continue the masquerade a little longer. In a moment they would enter the bar and she would reveal herself.

But two metres short of the doorway, Diego Montfalcó touched her arm again, this time for the purpose of halting her.

'Tell me something about them. How old is the *senyorita*, and what is she like?'

'Why do you want to know?' Although he had taken his hand away, Lucinda could still feel the light but firm pressure of his long fingers on her skin.

'I may have a job to offer her... if she's suitable.'

This was startling. She had assumed his visit must have to do with her grandfather, whose affairs were now her responsibility since her mother—Constantine's only child—had been barely on speaking terms with him.

'Perhaps it's better for you to judge for yourself, *senyor.*' She paused. Still speaking Catalan, she went on, 'I am Lucinda Radstone. Who gave you my name and address? Someone in London, presumably?'

'You are!' He looked very much taken aback, and visibly dismayed. 'Oh, no... you're far too young. I *have* wasted my time,' he said curtly. 'There's no point in even discussing it. Excuse me, please. I'm in a hurry with many urgent matters awaiting my attention. Good day.'

And with that he began to walk off, back to his opulent car.

Lucinda, however, had no intention of letting the matter rest there. Her instinctive liking for the man, based on his attractive and distinguished appearance, now became tinged with antipathy because of his curt dismissal of her as a candidate for the job, whatever it might be.

She was now the owner of the tumbledown *casita* in which Constantine Radstone had spent his last years, and had also inherited the shares which had been the source of a small, not to say minute, private income which had supplemented the old-age pension remitted to him from Britain. Without the pension he could not have spent the past ten years studying the plant and bird life of the delta of the great river Ebro, the Deltebre as it was known to the Catalans. Without the pension, which had stopped with his death, his granddaughter

couldn't continue to live in his cottage, much as she had
come to love it. She had a little money in the Banco
Central which would tide her over till Christmas.

But after that she would have to shut up the *casita*
and return to the workaday world and the colder climate
of northern Europe where the job prospects, if not good,
were better than they were here. She might even be forced
to sell the cottage, although she hoped not.

'Just a minute, *señor*,' she said firmly, switching to
the fluent *castellano* which had been one of her qualifications before her grandfather's letter, appealing for
help, had made her break off a career which had hardly
begun.

She knew that like all well-educated Catalans this man
would be equally at home with the country's principal
language, and she personally found it a more flexible
and subtle vehicle for her thoughts. There were indeed
many Spaniards who were opposed to the idea of one
country with two languages, particularly when a result—
perpetrated by extremists—was the defacing of Castilian
signs in Catalan areas.

'Don't you think,' said Lucinda, 'that it's a little im-
polite not even to explain what the work is of which I
am patently incapable?' As he checked his long stride,
she added, 'Surely the time it takes to drink a small *café
solo* won't make you seriously late? Ulldecona isn't very
far—especially in your fast car.'

Diego Montfalcó hesitated, clearly unwilling to linger
but perhaps aware that he had been somewhat cavalier.
He had a penetrating stare which now swept from the
top of her head to her slim sunburned feet shod in a
pair of cheap sandals from the Tuesday market in
Amposta, the nearest town of any size.

Perhaps he took her for even younger than eighteen,
and perhaps he remembered Angelita's reference to the

recent funeral. Whatever passed through his mind, it made him decide to turn back.

'You are right. Since we have met, I suppose I owe you some explanation,' he agreed. 'But I mustn't be long.' As they entered the bar, he added sardonically, 'Although I daresay I shall have to waste a good deal of time before the day is over. This country still has its own concept of punctuality.'

'That suggests you've lived abroad for some years,' said Lucinda.

'All my working life,' he answered, in English.

He spoke it with what her grandfather would have called an Oxford accent and it might have been an Englishman speaking, so perfect was his command of her native tongue.

'I'm an architect by profession...a job in which being on time and keeping other people up to scratch is crucially important. I soon lost the *mañana* attitude to time—if I ever had it. My formative years were spent in the charge of a kind but strict English nanny,' he explained.

This piece of information reinforced Lucinda's impression that he might be a member of Barcelona's *buena sociedad*, the élite social stratum which included direct descendants from the kings of Catalonia in the time, long ago, when the kingdom had spanned the Pyrenees and extended into part of what was now France. Certainly the name Montfalcó had a patrician ring about it, and there was elegance and good breeding in all the lines of his face and his tall lean body, and a hint of aristocratic hauteur in the curl of his nostrils and the cut of his mouth.

However, whatever his background, he showed no disdain for the rather crude ambience of the Bar Blau, its salami-coloured *terrazzo* floor littered with cigarette ends and sugar wrappers, and its barman unshaven and possibly unwashed as well. No doubt as well as being punctual, a successful architect had to be a good mixer, Lucinda reflected; as at ease among craftsmen and labourers as with important clients, and as much at home on a building site as in his own de luxe office.

'I don't like strong coffee,' he said, as the barman approached the table she had chosen. 'I'll have a *quinto*. And you? *Café solo?* Or a glass of wine?'

'Coffee with milk for me, please.'

Having given the order, Diego Montfalcó began a brisk explanation of his purpose in coming to see her.

'I am about to embark on a major project in Spain,' he began. 'Not the construction of a new building, but the repair of old ones...the restoration, in fact, of an entire village. A village which in recent years has become almost deserted as the young people left it and the older ones died off.'

Lucinda's eyes sparkled with interest, her recent annoyance forgotten, at least for the moment. 'I remember reading an article in *El Pais* about the large number of "ghost villages" all over Spain. There are hundreds of them, I believe?'

He nodded. 'Yes, and in a few cases efforts are being made to revive them. The one with which I'm involved is in the mountains not far from here. I shall be living on site for much of the time, at first in a makeshift fashion but before long, I hope, in some comfort. As soon as the house I'll be using is reasonably habitable, I shall be bringing my daughter to live in Spain. Rosa is seven years old. Her mother, who was English, is dead. For reasons I needn't go into the child speaks very little Spanish, and that must be remedied—quickly. I need someone to look after her and also to act as occasional assistant to me. Someone who is trilingual in English,

Spanish and Catalan. Such people aren't easy to find. When I was told that you were fluent in Spanish and had also learnt Catalan, I thought it worth coming to see you. But I was under the impression that you were a middle-aged spinster, not a young girl.'

'Perhaps I'm not as young as you think. I'm almost twenty-three,' she said, stretching the truth an iota because working in Spain would be so much better than having to go back to England where she had no relations and few other contacts. The *casita* didn't have a telephone and most of her former friends hadn't had time to keep in touch with her by letter, so gradually she had lost touch with the girls who had been students with her and the men she had dated. Among people in their early twenties, busy establishing careers, out of sight was soon out of mind, she had found. Most of them had thought her mad to come; giving up her good prospects to be an unpaid companion-help to an eccentric old man who chose to live miles from anywhere, studying migratory birds.

But in spite of her mother's dislike of him, Lucinda had loved her grandfather and knew that, had she not come, he wouldn't have finished his book and died a contented man. Their time together had been happy for him and for her and she didn't regret a moment of it.

'I took you for seventeen or eighteen,' said Diego Montfalcó. 'But even if you're twenty-two, you're still far too young. *Gracias——*' This to the barman as he brought their order.

The *quinto de cerveza* he had asked for was a fifth of a litre of beer, the smallest size bottle, which wouldn't take him long to drink. Lucinda knew she had very little time to persuade him to change his mind. Too little to spend any of it finding out who had misled him into thinking her a much older person. That question could keep until later . . . if there was a later.

Quickly she reeled off her various qualifications: the good French and passable German, the self-taught ability to type and cook nourishing meals and, latterly, to nurse an invalid.

'I also have a Spanish driving licence, which requires knowing something about how a car works as well as how to drive it,' she told him. 'It seems to me I'm almost ideally qualified for the post you want to fill. My only drawback is my age, and as far as your daughter's concerned I should think someone young would be more fun than an older woman—if indeed you can find someone older.'

'I shall have to,' he said, with a shrug. 'In the first place no one of your age would be happy living at Pobla de Cabres. There's nothing to do there at night. No TV . . . no one to talk to. The nearest bar is twenty kilometres away and the nearest disco even further. You'd quickly be bored to tears.'

'On the contrary, it would be the same sort of life I've been leading here—and I haven't been bored,' she retorted. 'I'm not the disco type. I should have thought you could see that.'

He gave her another thoughtful scrutiny. 'You do look the outdoor sports type, but even open-air girls like some after-dark fun at times . . . and young men to keep them company. The only young men at Pobla de Cabres will be workmen who, once the sun sets, will go back to wherever they live. They wouldn't be suitable companions for a girl like you in any case. In England it's different—quite a lot of the middle-class young are taking up skilled trades now. But that, to my knowledge, isn't happening in Spain. The middle class here is too new to be as relaxed about status as the English are nowadays.'

'The Deltebre doesn't abound in "suitable" men,' said Lucinda dryly. 'It hasn't bothered me here. Why should it anywhere else? I don't need a wild social life. I think I'm a natural loner...or perhaps it's fairer to say that I'd rather be on my own than with people who aren't on my wavelength. One is never alone with a good book,' she added, with a smile.

'Where do you get your books from?'

'My grandfather had a lot which I hadn't read when I came here. Now I've discovered a library in San Carlos de la Rápita.' This was another small town not far from the delta.

'There's no library within miles of Pobla de Cabres,' he pointed out.

'Probably not, but there must be a post office somewhere not too far away, or how will you get your mail? Quite often my mother sends me a parcel of books...enough to keep me going for several weeks.'

In telling him this, Lucinda was once more stretching the truth. Her mother, Georgia Garforth, the famous—some thought notorious—feminist writer and lecturer, did occasionally despatch a parcel of books she had read and didn't want to tote around with her. Forever on the move from one part of the globe to another, disseminating her message that it was no longer a man's world, Georgia no longer sent books, cast-off clothes and generous cheques as frequently as she had once done.

That was reasonable, thought Lucinda; a daughter of twenty-two should be able to fend for herself without much help from her mother. What hurt a little was the suspicion that Georgia would, at heart, have liked to break their connection entirely.

A grown-up daughter wasn't an asset to a woman whose lover was thirty-five while she, although she didn't look it yet, was almost ten years his senior. For all her forthright feminism, Georgia had always been vain—the kind of woman whose confidence depended on her striking looks as much as on her steel-sharp brain. When those looks began to go it would be a traumatic experience for her. Perhaps by ignoring Lucinda's birthdays she was trying to forget her own and the slow but inevitable decay of the compelling beauty which had helped to make her an international celebrity.

'Well, whether or not you're happy to spend your evenings reading, the fact remains that it won't do,' he told her flatly. 'Standards here are stricter than in northern Europe. It wouldn't be only your reputation which would suffer: I should also be seen in a bad light. Had you been the person I visualised, no one would have looked askance. But a girl of your age living in such isolation with a widower of my age would be sure to attract adverse comment. Nor would my client approve,' he added conclusively.

'Who is your client?' she asked, disappointed by the feeling that no argument was going to budge him, yet still curious to know who was behind the restoration of the village.

'I doubt if you would have heard of him. You've probably heard of his wife. She's a designer...Laurian.'

'Oh, yes—of course I have. I actually own one of her dresses. I didn't buy it, it was given to me. Will she be involved in the Pobla de Cabres project?'

'Possibly...later on...at the interior design stage. But that won't be for some time...not for a year or more.' He drained the last of his beer. 'Now, if you'll excuse me——' He rose to his feet.

Lucinda stood up to shake hands, an obligatory gesture on meeting and parting in Spain. Even teenagers did it.

'Won't you at least think it over?' she asked. 'I must get a job before long, and I'm sure you'd find me satisfactory.'

'I probably should, but too many eyebrows would be raised. If I were you, I should go home to England,' he advised her. 'Goodbye, Miss Radstone. Good luck.'

'Thank you...and good luck with your project,' she said, with a bright, strained smile.

As soon as his back was turned, her eyes glazed with sudden hot tears of profound disappointment. If only he had never come here...if only she had never heard of Pobla de Cabres! It was terribly frustrating to have a perfect solution to her problem so near at hand yet out of reach. She had very little hope he would change his mind. He struck her as a man of swift, fixed decisions; a rather didactic, austere man, in spite of that one charming smile.

Perhaps it was the loss of his wife which gave him the stern reserve of a much older man while still in his early thirties. Perhaps Señora Montfalcó had died fairly recently and he was still grieving for her, seeing the world as a wasteland as everyone must, for a time, after losing the person they loved most.

She herself felt lost and bereft, but the death of an aged grandparent was a mild grief compared with the loss of a beautiful young wife. For she would have been beautiful, Lucinda was certain of that.

She remembered reading—most of her knowledge came from books rather than direct experience—that married couples' looks were almost invariably of an equal standard. If that observation were accurate, Rosa Montfalcó's mother must have been outstandingly lovely to match her husband's princely bearing and finely sculptured features.

She watched him climb into his car and mustered a cheerful expression in case he should look back and wave. But he didn't. No doubt his thoughts had already moved on to his business in Ulldecona and he had dismissed her from his mind. Once he was back on the main road, the San Carlos bypass, the wild-goose chase to Sant Blai and a girl called Lucinda Radstone would be completely forgotten, she thought deflatedly, watching the luxurious car glide out of sight.

Later that day Lucinda began to pack up her few belongings.

After several hours' reflection, she had decided to take Diego Montfalcó's advice and go back to England; first to deliver the typescript of her grandfather's book to a suitable publisher, and then to resume the career plans put aside when Constantine wrote that he needed an amanuensis to help him complete his master-work.

He had been published before. Way back in the twenties and thirties he had been an explorer and climber, and had written a number of books describing his adventures, some of them still to be found on the shelves of second-hand bookshops. But his literary style was very dated and the adventures themselves had been superseded by the exploits of later explorers. His name and achievements were forgotten and his daughter's fame had not revived his reputation, because Georgia had long ago adopted her mother's maiden name and handed it down to her daughter.

The name on Lucinda's birth certificate was *Lucinda Mary Garforth* and, had she been born in early times, it would have been followed by *filia nullia*—nobody's child. Her parents had not been married.

Wedlock had been another tradition which Georgia had chosen to reject. It had been a mistake to get pregnant, she had told Lucinda, advising her to be more careful when she first fell in love with a man.

For Georgia readily conceded that love was a powerful emotion which happened to everyone sooner or later. Her view was not that it should be denied or avoided, but merely that love should never be allowed to deflect women from their chief purpose in life—which was not to keep house for a man or to bear and rear children. There had to be children, of course, if the human race was to survive. But giving birth, and training one's offspring to be self-sufficient as soon as possible, should always be secondary to a woman's career or vocation.

That was Georgia Garforth's credo.

If anyone argued that some women didn't want a career or have a vocation other than to make a haven of comfort and happiness for their loved ones, they would be firmly informed that this was only because of faults in the educational system which prevented many girls from finding their bent and developing their talents.

Wondering where her mother was now, and if she would ever tell her who her father was, Lucinda carefully folded the designer outfit which looked so incongruous hanging among the rest of her cheap chain-store clothes. Bought for Georgia's flamboyant lifestyle and worn only two or three times, the hand-smocked silk satin top and flowing crêpe-de-Chine pants, both labelled *Laurian*, seemed at present to have no place in Lucinda's wardrobe. She kept them for the pleasure of touching the beautiful fabrics and sometimes trying them on, hoping that, one day, she might have a chance to wear them in public. Even if one never went anywhere glitzy, it was a nice feeling to have something glamorous in reserve, just in case...

Having made up her mind to leave, she saw no point in delaying her departure. Every day a long-distance coach left the fishing port of San Carlos for the city of Barcelona. From there she might be able to get a cheap stand-by flight to London or, if not, continue by rail. In her absence, her nearest neighbours, Javier and Maria Roig, would keep an eye on the *casita*, and their youngest son, José-Maria, would drive her to the bus stop and then bring her grandfather's dilapidated old car back to the lean-to garage which had once been a stable for a mule.

As the sun began to sink towards the mountains west of the delta, Lucinda walked the kilometre to the Roigs' house. In summer the vast expanse of alluvial soil was green with growing rice. In winter it lay bare and desolate until the tractors came to plough it. Then, before Easter, the sluices would be re-opened and gleaming sheets of water would spread across the patchwork of fields to form an immense mirror which, almost every morning, reflected a spectacular sunrise and the dark silhouettes of the many birds which paused here on their way north.

The stark landscape of the delta was not to everyone's taste and sometimes, in winter, when a thick mist veiled the few trees and no one came down the lane for days at a time, Lucinda had felt pangs of loneliness. Yet she was sorry to leave. Spain—the real Spain, not the synthetic tourist resorts—was a country which captured the heart.

She knew she would often be homesick for the long, empty beaches, the distant sierras, the noisy restaurants, the sight of large close-knit families enjoying a picnic lunch in the olive groves of the hinterland on Sunday afternoons.

'Yes, it's better you go,' said Maria Roig, when Lucinda explained her intention to leave in the morning. 'Only today, in San Carlos, Javier heard of some houses

outside the town which had been robbed and van-
dalised. There have always been some thieves in Spain—
as there are everywhere, I daresay—but now there are
people who steal to buy drugs, and they are more
dangerous than ordinary thieves. It's not right for a
young, pretty girl to live on her own without a man to
protect her. Anything might happen.'

'I don't think there's very much risk of being robbed
or raped here on the *ribera*,' Lucinda replied. 'Thieves
look for houses with television aerials and other signs
of worthwhile loot. There's nothing of value in our
house; only books and a few ancient relics of my grandfather's travels as a young man.'

Having said goodbye to Maria—not for ever but
probably until the following summer when she might be
able to come back for a holiday—Lucinda returned to
the *casita* to have supper and go to bed early. She was
determined now to keep possession of the cottage. It
wasn't a valuable property which would fetch a sub-
stantial amount of money, so there seemed little point
in trying to sell it. And like the *Laurian* outfit, merely
to have a place in Spain, however ramshackle, would
give her a comfortable feeling if the coming winter in
England proved a severe one and she had to live in some
grotty furnished bed-sit.

Although the day had been warm, as darkness fell over
the delta it brought an autumnal chill. Lucinda decided
to light a fire, using the last of the driftwood she had
brought back from the beach last winter.

There was never any shortage of fuel for those with
the means to transport it back to their houses. She had
enjoyed hauling sea-bleached timbers back to the car
where her grandfather had sat on a deck chair, reading
and drinking the black-bottled Freixenet wine which,

because of protests from France, could no longer be marketed as *champaña*, although in Constantine Radstone's experienced opinion it was every bit as good as the cheaper non-vintage champagnes.

There was one bottle left in the cupboard. Lucinda thought she would have a glass, perhaps two, with her solitary supper. A thick bean-based soup was simmering on top of the bottled-gas stove as she laid a place at the table and started to open the wine. Before she had peeled away the foil, her ears caught the sound of a car approaching.

The unpaved lane passing the cottage wasn't one of the delta's main roads; the only person who used it at night was young José-Maria on his motorbike. The memory of his mother's warning that robbery and violence was becoming more widespread sent a tremor of unease down Lucinda's spine. She had never been nervous at night before, having no reason to be. However, as the car came nearer and finally stopped close at hand, she couldn't help feeling alarmed. Who would be visiting her at this hour? No one. No one she knew and could trust.

She heard the slam of a car door followed by some moments of silence and then footsteps on the path of paving slabs laid by her grandfather when he first came here. The path went right round the cottage, on the south side enlarging to form a terrace which in summer was shaded by a *parra*, a grape vine trained up the wall and over a series of bars to form a shady green canopy when the sun was at its fiercest.

Glad she had locked the door but doubtful if it would hold if someone tried to force it open, Lucinda crossed to the hearth and picked up the bayonet Constantine had used as a poker.

The loud rat-tat of the knocker made her stiffen apprehensively. But she tried to sound calm as she called out, *'Quién es?'*

'Diego Montfalcó.'

The intensity of her relief made her realise how frightened she had been. She hurried to the door and unlocked it, flinging it open, her grey-green eyes shining a welcome.'

'I'm sorry if I alarmed you.'

It was only then that she realised she was still gripping the bayonet, having transferred it to her left hand in order to unlock the door.

'Come in,' she said, standing back. 'Do I take it you've changed your mind?'

'No, I'm afraid not,' he answered. 'But I realised, during the day, that I should have asked about your circumstances . . . made sure you had the funds to go back to England. I'm spending the night in San Carlos. Would you care to come and have dinner with me?'

By Spanish standards it was still early evening. Nine o'clock was the earliest most people sat down to dine and many ate later than that.

'It's kind of you, Señor Montfalcó, but that would mean you would have to drive me home afterwards, and I'm sure you've done enough driving already today. Why not stay here and share my supper? There's more than enough for two and, although it's nothing elaborate, it's probably as good as anything you'll get in town. I was just going to have some bubbly, as my grandfather used to call it. Will you join me?'

'I'd be delighted. There's a new restaurant in San Carlos which I'm told is not bad, but it certainly won't be as restful as this pleasant room and a chair by the fire. Are you sure there's enough food for two?'

'Plenty...but it's very simple. A home-made soup, cold *tortilla* with *chorizo* and salad, a little *cabrales* which I bought from Angelita this morning, after you had gone. I'm almost a vegetarian, so I only go to her shop in the hope that she'll have some goat cheese.'

'It sounds a feast. May I deal with that for you?' he asked, with a nod at the opaque black bottle standing on the firelit table.

'If you would, please. I'll fetch another glass.'

Although he had crushed her hope that he had come back to offer her the job, Lucinda was still very pleased to see him. To spend her last night in Spain with an interesting companion was better than being on her own and wasting half the champagne. She couldn't have drunk the whole bottle.

When he had filled the glasses and handed one of them to her, Lucinda said, with a smile, 'Here's to Pobla de Cabres. I hope one day I'll be able to come back and see it.'

Diego Montfalcó acknowledged the toast with a courtly inclination of the head. Having sipped the champagne, he said, 'And here's to the successful publication of your grandfather's *magnum opus*, and also to your own success in whatever you take up next.'

'From what I hear of the shortage of jobs in England, I'll be happy to take up anything which will support me. I've decided to take your advice and go back at once. In fact, first thing tomorrow morning. I've arranged to be driven to the bus stop by the son of the people who will keep the *casita* aired for me.'

'Having made up your mind, you lose no time translating decision into action,' he remarked with a long, intent look.

The flickering light from the fire drew attention to the forceful bone structure under the taut olive skin now shaded, where his beard grew, by a darker tinge. Lucinda guessed he had risen early and shaved more than twelve hours ago, probably in Barcelona where he had told her he came from; meaning, she assumed, it was his birth-place and also his last stopping-place.

'Do sit down. The meal won't be long.' She took her glass to the kitchen where she wanted to add to the salad and cut more *chorizo* and bread.

When she returned to the living-room, her guest was not relaxing by the fire but looking at the closely-packed bookshelves which lined the two walls without windows.

'A catholic selection,' he remarked, speaking over his shoulder. 'Your grandfather's interests weren't limited to Spanish wildlife.'

'No, he had very wide interests.'

'Including feminism, I gather?' He took a volume from the shelf. 'It seems an unlikely ism to appeal to his generation. Or is this diatribe yours?' His tone was derogatory; she could see the curl of his lip as he looked at the photograph on the back of the dust-jacket.

'No, it belonged to my grandfather.'

She didn't add that the author of *Women: The Better Half* was Constantine's daughter and her mother.

For years Lucinda had been meeting people to whom Georgia's name was the proverbial red rag to a bull. She had learnt to lie low about their relationship. Not with everyone, but with many, it made *her* a suspect person. They took it for granted that she must share Georgia's views, including the more extreme ones. It had often been assumed by young men that Lucinda must be promiscu-ous. They soon found out that she wasn't, but eventu-ally their misapprehensions had become so tiresome that, on coming to Spain, she had decided to be known by her grandfather's surname. She would have taken her father's name had she known it, for it was clear that she had inherited her looks and much else from him.

'Grandfather didn't approve of it,' she added; an understatement, for the irate rumbles and exclamations of 'Tosh!' which had erupted from Constantine's wing chair as he read the first fifty pages of Georgia's clarion cry to females.

'I imagine not,' said the Spaniard, looking with dislike at the picture of Georgia acknowledging an ovation from the platform at a feminist rally. 'The woman is a virago... a psychological terrorist. At rock bottom her motivation isn't to improve life for women; it's to make trouble for everyone. What better way to wreck a stable society than to undermine the family unit? Taken to this extreme——' he gave the book a contemptuous flick with his fingertips '—feminism is anarchy.'

As always, when Georgia was castigated, Lucinda's instinct was to support her. In her teens she had sprung to her mother's defence with flushed cheeks and indignant denials of the charges against her. Maturity had taught her that a calmer reaction was more effective.

'I think that's going a bit far,' she said mildly. 'Have you actually read the book?'

'No—but I've heard her on TV and I've read her inflammatory articles. I've also had direct experience of the harm she does. Do you admire her?'

He looked so annoyed and so fierce that Lucinda might have hesitated to say yes even if it had been the honest answer. But in fact she did not admire Georgia or what she stood for. She had thought about it long and hard and come to the conclusion that none of the extreme measures taken by aggressive feminists had been necessary or effective in the slow advance to emancipation.

'No, I don't,' she said quietly. 'But I do think she's often misjudged and misrepresented…and I'm quite sure she isn't an anarchist.'

'She is an abomination.' He thrust the book back in its place. 'But we won't argue about her.' He began to question Lucinda about her grandfather's book and its publishing prospects.

Their conversation during supper ranged over a number of subjects. She learned that he had always specialised in the repair and conservation of ancient buildings, having found himself out of step with trends in contemporary architecture while he was qualifying.

'But an Englishman called Quinlan Terry has been having increasing success with buildings designed on classical principles, and I think we have passed the nadir of twentieth-century architecture and things are improving,' he told her. 'Not that I disapprove of all modern buildings. The glass-faced skyscrapers in America with their superb reflections are one of the wonders of our time. It's the dreary effect of unfaced, weather-stained concrete which I find unacceptably hideous. And some of the tile-faced blocks of *apartamentos* in Barcelona are very ugly, particularly when the canvas sun-blinds screening the balconies are in crude, glaring colours such as orange and royal blue. I'm afraid that Spain, like Britain, hasn't been well served by her architects in the past few decades.'

For the most part he talked and Lucinda listened, plying him with more *chorizo*—the last of a long, spicy sausage liked by her grandfather whose digestion had never failed him—and more of the soft leaf-wrapped goat cheese.

Unlike her mother, who dominated every conversation, Lucinda had always been a listener rather than a talker. This didn't make her willing to listen to bores.

If someone's talk wasn't interesting, she switched off. But her mind never wandered while Diego Montfalcó was talking. She found his mind and his face equally fascinating, and had to stop herself watching him too attentively.

It surprised her a little that tonight he was much less reserved than she had thought him in the morning. Perhaps it was the champagne which made him more forthcoming, or merely being able to relax at the end of a long busy day.

The town of Ulldecona, he told her, was a centre of furniture making. He had been there to investigate the production of high-quality fitments for the houses at Pobla de Cabres.

'Sit by the fire while I clear away and make coffee,' she suggested, when they finished eating.

He didn't offer to help her and she wondered how much, if at all, his years in London, married to an English wife, had changed the ideas he had grown up with. In general, here in Spain cooking and washing up was women's work. The men got together in bars while their meals were being prepared and afterwards they watched television. Probably the same basic customs prevailed among the *aristocracia* as among the peasantry and the expanding middle class.

The thought of Georgia's reaction to a man reclining at ease while a woman was busy in the kitchen made Lucinda smile to herself, as she washed the few dishes.

However, it was also a fact that her mother had no patience with women who, if their car broke down or an electrical fuse needed replacing, expected a man to deal with it. Her code was that every adult, male or female, should be able to cope with all life's simpler exigencies from ironing and mending clothes to changing a flat tyre.

When Lucinda returned to the living-room with two cups of coffee on a tray, she found her visitor lounging comfortably among the cushions on the shabby old sofa on the far side of the fireplace. His long legs were crossed at the ankle, his interlocked hands were resting on his flat stomach and his head was supported by the backrest. He was fast asleep.

For a time she sat opposite him, quietly drinking her coffee and studying the details of his recumbent form and unconscious face. His mouth hadn't fallen open, nor was he snoring gently as had been usual when Constantine Radstone napped.

Yet, sleeping, Diego Montfalcó did look different— younger and far less stressed. That he was under some kind of stress was something she hadn't pinpointed until now, seeing his face with the lines of tension smoothed away, his lips closed but not as firmly compressed as when he was awake and listening to someone else speaking.

Long black lashes fanned from his closed eyelids, the only feminine feature in an otherwise wholly masculine physiognomy of strong lines and hard planes.

When half an hour had passed and the fire needed replenishing if it were not to die down, she debated whether to rouse him or wait till he woke up naturally. But that might not be for two or three hours, and she had to make an early start in the morning and needed to go to bed herself soon.

At the same time she felt curiously reluctant to disturb him. He had mentioned during supper that he hadn't yet checked in at the Miami Park, the only good hotel in San Carlos. But at this time of year it wasn't likely to be full, however late he turned up, and in that improbable event there was the state-owned *parador* at

Tortosa, an ancient city on both banks of the Ebro some way upriver from the delta but not more than half an hour's run in his BMW.

Yet if she didn't wake him up it was very unlikely he would sleep through the night. The room would grow cold when the fire died and he would wake, stiff and chilled, some time in the small hours.

Feeling, after some thought, that she must wake him now, she rose from her chair and went to shake him gently by the arm. The movement had no effect: he was very heavily asleep, almost as if he had taken a sedative.

Lucinda shook him more vigorously, but still without result. Then she remembered reading that to pinch the lobe of their ear was a good way to wake someone. A little reluctant to touch a stranger so intimately, she took the lobe of his left ear between her finger and thumb, gently pressing rather than nipping it.

At first nothing happened. Then, when she repeated the pressure, his eyelids twitched but didn't open.

'Katie...' he murmured. 'Katie...' A smile flickered round his mouth.

Lucinda withdrew her hand and took a hasty step backwards. Every instinct told her that, by touching him in that way, she had triggered a memory of the girl he had lost. He was no longer deeply asleep but dreaming of his dead wife; she could tell it by his expression. All at once he looked happy, his wide mouth curving at the corners as his subconscious conjured up a time which was gone for ever, a time before tragedy hit him.

For him to wake now would be terrible, she thought. To be confronted by someone who wasn't Katie...to realise that Katie would only ever come back to him in dreams...such an awakening must be unbearably painful.

Holding her breath, she prayed that she wouldn't have to witness the cruel return to reality. It wasn't until several minutes later when, to her relief, he appeared to be sleeping soundly again, that she realised she had tears in her eyes—again.

As it wasn't the time of the month which was making her emotional, it must have something to do with re-action to her grandfather's death, thought Lucinda. Or maybe it was just that the end of a loving marriage was enough to make any sensitive person weep a little. She felt in her bones that Diego Montfalcó was the kind of man who, once having given his heart to a woman, would love her with passionate intensity and never fully re-cover from losing her.

Was the little girl, Rosa, like her? Was that why he looked so strained? Because his seven-year-old daughter was an ever-present reminder of his dead wife?

She felt a sharp ache of pity for him; a man with so much going for him—brains, breeding, looks—even, fleetingly, charm, although this last must be only a shadow of the vital magnetism it had once been. But none of those assets counted if his heart was so shriv-elled with pain that he no longer had the capacity to feel anything but despair.

With a sigh, she built up the fire with two large silver-grey logs, then placed the spark guard in front of it. On one arm of the sofa was a travelling rug her grandfather had wrapped round himself when taking a daytime nap. She unfolded it and draped it lightly over the Spaniard's legs. Next she wrote a note for him to find when he woke.

Tried to wake you but couldn't. Stay the night, if you like. I'll be getting up at 6 a.m.

L.R.

The source of light at the *casita* was a solar panel on

the roof which powered a twelve-volt battery from which to run fluorescent tubes and, if it was wanted, a television. Tonight, however, there had been enough radiance from the flames to make the harsher light unnecessary and they had eaten supper in the pleasant old-fashioned glow of firelight.

In case this had dwindled too much for her note to be readable by the time he woke up, Lucinda fetched a candle from a cupboard. It wasn't one of the ordinary household candles she kept on hand for emergencies but a much thicker cylinder of wax contained in a crimson plastic casing, the kind of candle that Spanish people brought at Christmas time to burn at shrines and in churches.

Striking a match, she touched the flame to the wick and, when it was burning steadily, placed the candle on the ledge high above the hearth and propped the note against it.

Then she tiptoed away to her bedroom leading off the central hallway.

It was five forty-five when the alarm clock went off. After extending an arm to stop the low-pitched buzzer, Lucinda spent a few minutes enjoying the cosy nest under the duvet. Then, fearful of falling asleep again, she felt for the switch of her reading light, flung back the feather-light quilt and bounced quickly out of bed.

It wasn't until she had brushed her long hair and fastened it back from her face with two plastic butterfly spring-clips that she remembered she wasn't alone in the house. Or hadn't been when she went to bed. Perhaps she was now.

Pulling a honey-coloured robe over her pale green cotton-knit sleeping suit—in summer she slept in her skin—she tied the sash round her waist. Her feet were already snug in the cheap fur-lined rabbitskin bootees to be found in every Spanish market throughout the cooler months.

The red Christmas candle was still burning steadily on the mantelshelf. But the sofa was no longer occupied. The rug had been folded and replaced on the arm, the squashed cushions shaken out.

He had gone and not even scribbled a note of farewell on the back of her note to him, she discovered disappointedly. Perhaps he had been annoyed at waking up at whatever time he had woken. It was odd she hadn't heard the car start up.

Would she ever see him again? Perhaps, if she came back to Spain next summer and made a point of finding out where Pobla de Cabres was and going there to seek him out. But why did she want to see him again? They were only chance acquaintances... ships that passed in the night. Except that he might have employed her had she been forty-two instead of twenty-two, they had no point of contact. He was just an interesting man who, for a few hours, had touched her heart. But only with compassion... nothing more. How could it have been anything more?

The sudden sound of water running made her snatch in her breath. Spinning round, she saw that the kitchen door, which she had left open, was now closed, with fine slivers of light showing round its edges.

He hadn't left after all. He was still here... making himself a cup of tea, perhaps.

Conscious of an absurd degree of relief that she hadn't lost the chance to say goodbye to him, Lucinda hurried to the kitchen and opened the door. Had the tap been running in the bathroom, she would have knocked before catching him unaware. But in fact it was she, not Diego

Montfalcó, who was the more surprised when they confronted each other.

There was nothing wrong with his nerves. Although she had opened her bedroom door quietly and her slippered feet had made no sound on the threadbare Oriental rugs which her grandfather had spread on his floors, the man in the kitchen gave no sign of being startled by her sudden appearance in the doorway.

It was she who recoiled and stammered an apology.

For he wasn't making a cup of tea. Stripped to the waist, his chest and shoulders unexpectedly muscular for a man whose occupation wasn't physically strenuous, he was in the process of removing the stubble from his cheeks and chin. One side of his face was still covered with lather, the other one was already shaved.

'Good morning,' he said. 'I thought if I shaved and washed in here, it would leave the bathroom free for you. The kettle will boil in a moment. Do you like tea or coffee first thing?'

'Good morning. Er...tea for me, please. I'm sorry I didn't knock.'

'Why should you?' he said, with a shrug, before continuing to shave.

'Did you sleep right through till this morning?' Lucinda asked.

'I woke about two o'clock, read your note and decided it wasn't worth going to the hotel for what remained of the night. So I made myself comfortable on the sofa, set the alarm on my watch for half past five and went back to sleep,' he said, between sweeping strokes of the razor.

'I hope the rug was enough for you. I ought to have put out a blanket and a proper pillow.'

'The fire was still going when I woke up. The room was still warm when I woke for the second time.' He rinsed lather from his blade. 'But you should have made more strenuous efforts to wake me and send me packing. It wasn't sensible to allow me to spend the night here.'

'You worry too much about what people will think,' she answered. 'Anyway, no one is going to know you were here all night. I doubt if the Roigs, my nearest neighbours, would have heard your car arriving. They have their TV going full blast all evening until the programmes close down.'

'I wasn't concerned with that, but with something far more important—your safety,' he told her. 'Did you lock your bedroom door, or push something heavy against it?'

'No: I didn't think it was necessary. You aren't the sort of man who attacks defenceless women.'

'How can you be sure?'

'I don't know...I just am. If I'd had any doubts I shouldn't have asked you to supper. I'd have made an excuse to go outside and run like hell to the Roigs' place.'

Her answer amused him. The fugitive charm she had glimpsed when he smiled at her yesterday reappeared like a brief spell of sunlight on a cloudy day.

'Girls can't be too careful these days. Not all rapists look brutes, and some very nasty murderers have seemed to be charming at first.'

'I know, and I am aware of the risks,' she assured him. 'But it's also true that one can be *too* nervous and suspicious. Although you wouldn't think so from reading the papers and watching TV, there are still more good, kind people in the world than the other sort. If you remember, your motive in coming back here was that you were concerned about whether I had the money to get back to England.'

'Yes, it was—and I meant to discuss your situation more fully last night, but somehow we ended up talking about other things.'

When he bent over the sink to cup his hands under the running tap and rinse the remaining streaks of lather from his face, the muscles of his back shifted and rippled under his smooth unblemished skin which, had he spent the summer in his homeland, would no doubt have been deeply tanned. Even so, it wasn't the pallid white of a northerner's skin but an attractive golden colour, making her want to reach out and touch it.

Lucinda had always been responsive to textures, but the impulse to stroke him surprised her. She realised that, for the first time in her life, she was in the grip of a powerful physical attraction. It was both exciting and disturbing.

He reached for a small red towel lying on the grey marble worktop beside his red wetpack. Having dried his face, he said, 'As it happens I'm going back to England myself today. As you've trusted me to spend the night here, will you trust me to drive you to London? Or, if you dislike long journeys by road, I can run you as far as Barcelona. But you'd actually be doing me a favour if you came all the way. I get very bored on my own and there isn't always something worth listening to on the radio.'

A wave of surprise and delight washed over her, leaving her speechless. She had not felt like this for years, not since the one occasion when, unexpectedly, Georgia had turned up for the school prize-giving at which Lucinda had received a silver cup for the best essay, in French, on a subject set by the headmistress. It had been the only occasion when Georgia had been there to applaud her achievements, but it had made up for all the other times when she had said she would come but had failed to appear.

'It's terribly kind of you,' she exclaimed. 'But are you *sure* you want a travelling companion?'

'Perfectly sure. That's settled, then. I have very little luggage with me. There's plenty of room for anything you'd like to take with you but wouldn't have taken otherwise.'

'Thank you. I'll go and have a quick shower, and afterwards I'll cook us some breakfast.'

'Off you go, then. I'll deal with the kettle,' he said, as it began to whistle.

A few minutes later, standing under a jet of water hand-pumped from an underground *cisterna* and heated by butane gas, Lucinda acknowledged to herself that, between mid-morning and midnight yesterday, she had fallen in love.

In a way it filled her with joy that at long last the first great experience of a woman's life was happening to her. But, while it made her heart beat faster to think that instead of saying goodbye she was going to be travelling all the way to England with him, her common sense told her that loving Diego Montfalcó was very unlikely to lead to happiness.

Deep, incurable heartache seemed a more probable outcome.

In the first place he wasn't heart-free, but haunted by a marriage which had ended in tragedy. And as well as that reason why he was unlikely ever to care for Lucinda, or perhaps any woman, there was another obstacle between them.

Although he didn't know it yet, she was Georgia Garforth's daughter, and he had made it very clear that Georgia was one of his *bêtes noires*.

CHAPTER TWO

WHILE Diego was packing the car and Lucinda was at the Roigs' house, explaining that she wouldn't be catching the bus because a friend had offered her a lift, a glorious apricot sunrise had come up out of the sea, suffusing the lofty crags of the Sierra Montsía, the mountains behind San Carlos, in a soft rosy glow.

Now they were on their way, crossing the sunlit Ebro by the wide new bridge, with a view of the old narrow bridge and the town of Amposta on their left, a little way upstream.

A short distance further on they came to a fork where most of the traffic veered right to follow the ordinary coast road, but Diego took the other direction which was the entrance to the *autopista*.

As he slowed down for Lucinda to take a ticket from the machine by the toll booth, he gave her a smiling glance and said, 'Next stop Paris.'

Then the car began to pick up speed and in a matter of moments, it seemed to her, they were surging along at nearly eighty miles an hour. Although she wouldn't have guessed they were travelling so fast if she hadn't glanced at the dials on the dashboard. Eighty in the luxurious comfort of the BMW was a smoother run than going forty in her grandfather's ancient runabout.

Did Diego—she had long since stopped thinking of him as Señor Montfalcó—really mean to drive straight through to Paris? she wondered. Surely, even at this speed, it was too great a distance to travel without a rest? A proper rest, not just a meal-stop.

As if he read the thought in her mind, he said, 'Actually we shan't be stopping in Paris. The distance from here to Calais is roughly a thousand miles——'

For a nasty moment Lucinda thought he was going to say they would be driving straight through to the Channel port. Her stomach churned at the thought of what his reaction would be like, in an emergency, after being at the wheel for...how many hours?

'—and there are people who do the journey in one mad belt up the motorway,' he continued. 'I think that's stupid and dangerous. Even in a fast car there's a limit to how long one can drive without losing one's alertness. I propose to spend tonight at Lyon, which is approximately half-way to the French coast, and where there's a very fine restaurant—one of the best in all France—where we can have a good dinner.'

I should have known he wasn't the type to risk his life, and mine, by driving for longer than is safe, thought Lucinda. Aloud, she said, 'That sounds lovely, except that I'm not sure I'm suitably dressed for a fashionable restaurant.'

The *Laurian* outfit was a bit over the top for dining in public, she felt. It was meant for a black tie occasion, or a very special dinner *à deux*, and it called for a gala hairdo. It wasn't right for tonight.

Diego glanced sideways at her, taking in her travelling clothes.

Had she been going by coach, she would have worn her track suit and trainers. Coming with him, in his elegant car, she had chosen to wear the feminine equivalent of his clothes. He was wearing an open-collared shirt under a cashmere sweater, fine beige gabardine trousers, silk socks and well-polished loafers the colour of chestnuts. His lightweight tweed sports coat, in which she had glimpsed the label of one of the most illustrious

men's tailors in London, was lying on the back seat for
when he got out of the car.

Her own clothes were not of the same superior quality
as his, but they were similar in style, all classics bought
for long wear. She had found out early in life that on a
limited budget it wasn't possible to follow fashion; even
very cheap clothes were expensive if they went out of
style in a few months. Colours, too, had their draw-
backs, although it had often been tempting to splurge
on a vivid scarlet or a subtle shade of blue. Lucinda's
natural colouring allowed her to wear most colours and
her particular favourites were soft greens which brought
out the tiny flecks in her irises, and peach which flattered
her skin. However in spite of these preferences she almost
always stuck to neutrals because flannel grey, tan and
navy made mixing and matching easier and gave clothes
a lot more mileage.

'You look very well dressed to me. What you have on
now is fine,' said Diego, after swiftly appraising her
cream blouse and natural lambswool sweater combined
with a pleated wool skirt in a small houndstooth check.

'Thank you.' She wondered what he really thought.
An architect must have a more critical eye for women's
clothes than the average man. Did he think, privately,
that she looked dull, lacking in pizazz? Perhaps not, as
his own taste was conservative.

In a very short time they were sweeping past the provincial capital, the seaside city of Tarragona.

'I've never been there,' said Lucinda. 'Soon after I
came to Spain my grandfather was well enough for us
to drive down to Granada—he wanted to show me the
Alhambra. After that holiday together his health began
to deteriorate and we never went far afield again.'

'There's a lot of this country I don't know either,'
said Diego, as they flashed past a huge lorry exporting

Spanish produce to northern Europe. 'And large parts of England I've never had time to visit. Most of my work has been in the Cotswolds and the West Country.'

She was on the point of asking how a Catalan from Barcelona had come to work in England when it struck her that the answer might very well have to do with his marriage to an English girl, and that was a subject better left alone.

'You still haven't told me who it was who mentioned me to you in the first place,' she reminded him.

'It was an elderly man—an architect by profession, an ornithologist by inclination—I met at the private view of an exhibition of architectural drawings,' he explained. 'We got into conversation and I told him about the Pobla de Cabres project. Apparently he and your grandfather corresponded about birds. I must have mentioned that I needed a trilingual person to help with my daughter and my work, because several days later he rang up and read out some extracts from a letter from your grandfather.'

'He had quite a number of pen-friends. He used to write to them at night, and his failing eyesight and the tremor in his right hand made his writing quite hard to read sometimes,' said Lucinda. 'Also he was a great one for crossing out and scribbling in afterthoughts. He could have dictated his letters to me, but I don't think he realised how muddled and illegible many of them were. I imagine what happened was that he mentioned his granddaughter and the "grand" got crossed out, leaving "daughter"!'

'Very probably. Anyway, it doesn't matter. Coming to see you wasn't far out of my way and was rather well timed, as it turned out.'

'A godsend for me,' she agreed warmly. 'This is much nicer than hanging about at the airport, waiting for a stand-by, or thirty-six hours on a coach, which is the way I came down here.'

On the south side of Barcelona they stopped for petrol and coffee.

"Do your parents live in Barcelona?' she asked, as they were walking back to the car.

'Yes, but I saw them on my way south and they know I haven't time to call in on the way back. I only came down by road because there were some fragile things my mother wanted brought from England. Otherwise it would have been more convenient to fly and borrow their car for a couple of days. Do I gather that you've lost your parents?'

'My father—yes,' she replied, wondering how he would react to being told that she didn't even know her father's name. 'My mother travels a lot. We don't see much of each other.'

She wondered if she ought to be frank with him and say who her mother was. But wasn't it wiser to wait until it was firmly established that she herself had no leanings towards militant feminism?

On the north side of Barcelona the landscape began to change, becoming noticeably greener and more wooded. By mid-morning they were at the frontier between the small towns of La Junquera on the Spanish side and Le Boulou on the French side of the Pyrenees.

'If it's all right with you, I'm going to stop in Le Boulou to buy the makings of a picnic,' said Diego, when they had been waved through the police and Customs barriers. 'If we're going to be feasting tonight, we don't need much at midday, but the snacks on sale at the service stations are never very appetising.'

'A picnic would suit me perfectly,' she agreed. 'It looks as if France is having good weather at present.' The sky on the northern side of the mountains was as clear and blue as it had been since they crossed the Ebro.

Evidently Diego had shopped in Le Boulou before. In a very short time they were back at the car with a loaf of *pain integral*, three different sorts of French cheese and a bag of apples. He spoke excellent French, she had noticed, and had a nice way with the two old ladies who had served him.

Having set out early, they had lunch early; eating it at an open-air table at one of the many picnic areas alongside the *autoroute*.

By this time they were skirting the Golfe du Lion corner of the Mediterranean, still within sight of the sea in places, with an inland view of arid moorlands covered with thorny *garrigue*.

Although other picnickers there were drinking wine with their food, Diego had not bought any, which Lucinda thought was sensible of him. On such a hot day even a small amount of wine could make one drowsy and, coming through Spain, she had noticed a clever poster: a drawing of a glass of wine, then a plus sign, then a car and the sign for equals followed by an ambulance. No caption was necessary.

Before lunch they quenched their thirst with water from a drinking fountain and later they stopped for coffee at a service station.

It was during this stop that Diego said, 'Would you like to drive for a while?'

Lucinda was amazed that he should offer her the opportunity. The only man she had known well was her grandfather who, latterly, had had no choice but to let her drive his car. He might not have done so when younger. It was her impression that most men considered themselves much better drivers than women. The last thing she had expected was for Diego to suggest she should take the wheel of his high-powered and costly car.

'You don't have to,' he added, when she didn't reply. 'I'm not at all tired, but being a passenger can be rather boring over long distances, so I thought you might like to take over for an hour or so.'

'I should love to, but I must tell you that I've never driven anything but small cars.'

'Don't let that worry you. A bigger car isn't harder to handle...it's usually easier because the braking and steering is better than on the smaller, cheaper models. I might have had reservations about letting you try mine out in the centre of Paris,' he admitted drily, 'but on the *autoroute* you shouldn't have any problems.'

So, not without some trepidation although she strove not to show it, Lucinda adjusted the driving seat to suit her shorter legs and listened attentively to Diego's brief explanation of the controls, which were different from those on the car she was used to. Then she cautiously rejoined the unceasing shuttle of traffic which, here in France, made the Spanish *autopista* seem almost deserted by comparison.

That he genuinely felt no anxiety about letting her drive was proved when, a short time later, he said, 'I think I will have a zizz,' and adjusted the passenger seat into a reclining position.

'Would you like the radio turned off?' asked Lucinda. On leaving the last stopping place he had tuned in a French station which was playing light music.

'No, leave it on. I like it.' He eased his long frame into a more relaxed posture and closed his eyes.

Several times when they were driving on parts of the Spanish *autopista* with no other traffic in sight Lucinda had seen the speedometer needle creep past the ninety mph mark. With Diego at the wheel she would not have been worried if it had gone to a hundred. But she had no desire to 'do a ton' herself and felt that seventy was quite fast enough while she was in charge.

Earlier she had flipped through a book called *Gastronomic Routes of France*, which was in the pocket of the nearside door, and studied the route they were following. Presently the blue and white signs at the roadside indicated that they had swung away from the coast and would soon be following the Rhône, one of the great rivers of France, upstream to Lyon.

There was something curiously intimate about travelling across Europe in a car with one other person. Lucinda found it hard to believe that the day before yesterday she hadn't know that the man beside her existed. Already it felt as if she had known him for ever; and perhaps, in a way, she had.

Didn't every girl, from the time she was old enough to think about love, spend her life waiting for *him* to show up? Even if she had never been sure what he would look like, she had known some things about him...that he would be kind and generous, a man who laughed easily, who liked most of the same things that she liked even if they had some separate interests, a man who would be her friend as well as her lover.

At college Lucinda had known girls who fell in love with men who lacked all those qualities; men who were stunningly attractive but also selfish and thoughtless, men who couldn't be trusted. She had felt certain she would never be swept away by a purely physical attraction. True love was much more than that, she had always believed.

Yet now, on the face of it, she seemed to have done precisely what she had vowed never to do: fallen headlong in love with a good-looking stranger—a foreigner to boot.

Yes, I have, she admitted to herself, flicking a swift upwards glance at the ruins of a mediaeval castle perched on the crest of a crag. But already I know there's a lot more to him than a handsome face.

For a few seconds she took her eyes off the road again to look at the face in question, now half turned away so that all she could see were the lines of his temple and cheekbone and the angle of his strong jaw.

Returning her attention to the road, she remembered the brief telephone call Diego had made from Le Boulou. Standing outside the kiosk, not intending to listen in, she couldn't help hearing him reserve a table at the restaurant where he wanted to dine. She gathered he had been lucky to get one, having rung up a few minutes after a cancellation.

Upon reflection she felt sure that, had he planned to travel north today, he wouldn't have left booking a table until this morning, not if the place was one of the best in France. A suspicion was growing in her that he was taking her back to England out of chivalrous concern for her situation, not because he had intended to travel back today.

Is it possible that he's drawn to me as I'm drawn to him? she wondered hopefully. Or is that wishful thinking?

Having slept for about forty minutes, Diego woke up, glanced at his watch and looked about to see where they were. But he remained in a recumbent position, apparently content to let her continue driving for as long as she wished.

Shortly before he awoke the French disc jockey had introduced an album made by one of Lucinda's favourite singers, Charles Aznavour. He had just finished one of his most famous songs, *She*, and now was beginning the haunting *Somewhere*.

'...I know I'll find somewh——'

The romantic lyric was abruptly interrupted as Diego snapped off the radio.

'One can have enough of that, don't you think?'

He selected a tape from a selection under the dashboard, slotted the cassette into place and pressed the start button. Lucinda recognised the opening notes of Tchaikovsky's Violin Concerto.

Why had he cut off the Aznavour song? Because he couldn't stand more than a certain amount of pop? Or because that particular song conjured up painful memories? Because the words were a reminder that he had found love...and lost it?

Between Valence and Vienne they again stopped for coffee and to stretch their legs, after which Diego resumed the driving.

Reminded of his small daughter by a French child in the back of a car they passed, Lucinda said, 'Your little girl is seven, I think you said. Will she mind being transplanted...leaving her present school?'

'Rosa hasn't started school yet. Unfortunately a lot of her life has been spent in and out of hospital,' he answered. 'When she was three she was very badly scalded. Her recovery was a long business involving several skin grafts. She'd been to play-school for a short time before the accident, but at five she was still too ill to start proper school. When she was fit to start, it seemed better for her to have private tuition for a time to help her catch up what she'd missed. I was starting to look for a school when the Pobla de Cabres project came up.'

'I see. Who looks after Rosa when you're away?'

'Up to now, Mrs Boston, my housekeeper. But her unmarried sister isn't well and needs her to keep house for her. Otherwise I should have asked Mrs Boston to come to Pobla de Cabres with us, and I think she would have agreed. She's sixty-something, but very adaptable. However, her sister's need is greater than ours. Mrs Boston is only waiting for me to make alternative arrangements and she'll be off.'

Lucinda was tempted to point out that, but for his scruples about her age, he had an alternative to hand. However, she thought better of it. She had already urged him to think over giving her the job. To press her case might do more harm than good.

'My mother would like to have Rosa with her in Barcelona,' Diego went on. 'She'd certainly be well cared for and have several cousins to play with. But she wants to stay with me, and I think that would be best, at least for the next year or two. She's had enough traumas in her life. I am her sheet-anchor.'

And perhaps she is yours, thought Lucinda, her eyes on his long supple fingers resting lightly on the wheel.

It was mid-afternoon when they drove into the city of Lyon, famous, she knew, for its cuisine and for the silks woven there.

Diego's choice of hotel was an old-fashioned but comfortable establishment where he asked for two single rooms with private baths. Before they separated, she to be taken upstairs and he to put the car in the lock-up garage, he said, 'Will it suit you to meet down here in, say, fifteen minutes and go for a stroll—and that glass of wine we didn't have at lunchtime? I shan't be driving any more today. Tonight we'll go by taxi.'

'That would be fine. Fifteen minutes,' Lucinda agreed, checking her watch.

In the bedroom to which she was shown, she unpacked her small overnight bag and hung up the shirt she had meant to put on tomorrow but would now change into tonight. She could also exchange the unob-

trusive studs she wore in her ears everyday for a pair of
gold hoops, and wear her grandmother's peacock
pendant, a beautiful piece of Art Nouveau jewellery with
carved opal 'eyes' in the bird's tail and an opal drop
hanging below it. That, if nothing else about her, would
be worthy of the occasion.

'*Merci, madame. Au revoir.*'

Having paid the bill with a credit card, Diego bowed
to the proprietress, picked up his grip and led the way
along the passage which led to the hotel's garage.

Following him, Lucinda was thinking that last night's
dinner at the restaurant of Paul Bocuse, one of France's
master chefs, was probably the most superb meal she
would ever eat in her life; unforgettable not only for the
black truffle soup and the *Volaille de Bresse* but because
she was in love with the man on the other side of the
table.

This morning's breakfast of hot flaky croissants, black
cherry jam and wonderful coffee in thick pottery cups
had been equally memorable, even though Diego had
talked to the waitress more than to her. But already both
dinner and breakfast had passed into memory, and now
her time with him was running out. By tonight they
would have said goodbye. After finding a room in a
cheap hotel, she would probably eat in the nearest fast
food place. Rather a comedown after *chez* Bocuse.

She wouldn't mind that as much as parting from him.
Emily Brontë had experienced what she was feeling now
and written a poem about it. '*Once drinking deep of
that divinest anguish, How could I seek the empty world
again?*'

As Diego unlocked the boot and disposed of their
baggage, she said, 'I shall have to settle up with you in
pounds, not having any francs. I should have changed

some money at the border yesterday, but we were waved
through so quickly I forgot I should need some French
currency.'

He didn't embarrass her by refusing her offer
altogether, but he wouldn't allow her to pay for her share
of their dinner.

Yesterday's lovely weather had changed to overcast
skies and a chilly little wind as they set out for Paris.
As it had north of Barcelona, after Lyon the countryside
changed; the houses and farms looked different as well
as the landscape. They had re-entered northern Europe
where already the trees had lost most of their leaves, and
the sense of a long, dark winter about to close down
made Lucinda even more depressed.

Diego was also preoccupied and they had little conversation on the run to Paris, where the hair-raising lane-
changing of French drivers on the *boulevard
périphérique*, carrying four lanes of northbound through
traffic, made her glad she wasn't at the wheel.

Again they had a picnic lunch from provisions bought
before leaving Lyon, including a delicious *pâté de
campagne*. But they had to eat in the car, with the rising
wind and flurries of rain making an alfresco meal
impossible.

'I was hoping to cross the Channel by hovercraft, but
they won't be running if this keeps up,' said Diego,
peeling a pear for her. 'Are you a good sailor?'

'I don't honestly know. I've only been on the ferry
once and the sea was flat calm that day.'

It was anything but calm when they reached Calais.
By that time the wind was a gale and both sea and sky
were dark grey, the churning sea flecked with white and
huge waves buffeting the docks and sending up showers
of spray. But it wasn't yet rough enough to stop the
ferries running.

Diego made Lucinda take an anti-seasick pill which he'd bought from a chemist on their way through the town. Perhaps she didn't take it soon enough for it to be effective, or perhaps it would have worked if she hadn't had *pâté* for lunch. Scarcely had the ferry left harbour than she had to excuse herself and beat a hasty retreat to the Ladies.

The next hour and a half was a nightmare. She had never felt so ill in her life. At some stage of the ordeal, a stewardess asked her name and told her a gentleman outside was concerned about her.

Wishing she could die, Lucinda said faintly, 'Tell him...I'm fine...just a bit...queasy. I—I'll see him when we get there.'

If I live that long, she thought miserably, before she was overwhelmed by another racking bout of sickness.

When at last the ferry docked, she and a great many others emerged from the ship's lavatories with the telltale greenish-white pallor of the victims of *mal de mer*.

Diego was waiting to shepherd her down the car deck when the call came for motorists to return to their vehicles. He was one of the few passengers who showed no sign of being affected by the crossing.

'Poor you! I'm sorry that coming back with me inflicted that on you,' he said sympathetically, putting an arm round her shoulders and giving her a comforting hug.

Lucinda was still feeling terrible and hating being in a crowd as more and more people gathered to go below. She longed to turn her face into his shoulder and burst into tears of exhaustion, but she managed to muster a wan smile.

'Would you please put that cigarette out?' he said curtly to a youth who had just lit up, and so steely was his tone that the command was obeyed without demur.

Diego kept his arm protectively round her as they went down the companionways and he helped her into the car. It was almost worth being ill to enjoy his solicitude.

She began to feel better when, having driven ashore, he reached across to touch the button which lowered her window and let in a little fresh air. It wasn't raining in Dover, nor was the wind as rough as it had been when they left France.

On the outskirts of the town he stopped at a hotel and Lucinda remembered it had been his intention to have dinner before driving to London. The thought of food was repellent to her, but she realised he must be hungry.

However, Diego said to the receptionist, 'My companion has just endured a very bad crossing from Calais. Is there somewhere quiet where she can have some dry biscuits, coffee and brandy?'

'Yes, sir... certainly, sir. There's a nice fire in the lounge, and you'll probably have it to yourselves as most people use the bar or the television room. It's the first on the left. I'll send the lounge waiter to you right away.'

'You need a proper meal,' said Lucinda. 'Don't feel you must stay with me. I'll be quite happy on my own while you're having dinner.'

'I had something coming over.'

'You ate!' she exclaimed in amazement.

'It was rather a comedown after last night,' said Diego drily.

His choice of phrase was a reminder of how little time there was left before they went their separate ways. Not wanting him to remember her—if he remembered her—looking a mess, she said, 'If you'll excuse me, I'll go and freshen up a bit.'

Even in the flattering pink light of the hotel's powder room, she looked very washed-out, with this morning's careful make-up reduced to smudges of mascara under her eyes. She removed them and re-did her eyes and put on some lipstick. It made her look slightly better.

When she went to the lounge, the things Diego had ordered for her were on a low table beside the cheerful coal fire, but he wasn't. She poured out a cup of coffee and cautiously nibbled a Bath Oliver.

Diego reappeared. 'I've asked Mrs Boston to prepare the spare room and organise a light supper. You may not think so at the moment, but by the time we reach London you'll be hungry.'

'But I can't impose on you,' she protested. 'You've already been more than helpful.'

'It won't be an imposition. You can't spend your first night in England alone in an hotel after what you've been through.'

Relief welled inside her. Reprieved!

'It's terribly kind of——' she began.

He cut short her thanks. 'Drink some brandy. It will put you to rights faster than anything.'

To her surprise, it did. By the time they set off on the last lap, she was feeling herself again. Although perhaps it was not having to say goodbye yet, as much as the brandy, which made her feel better.

'What part of London do you live in?' she asked him.

'Near Liverpool Street Station.'

Close to a mainline station and on the fringe of the East End seemed an odd place for an architect to live.

Diego must have guessed what she was thinking. He said, 'In an area called Spitalfields, which is now rather fashionable but wasn't when I discovered it. It's through living there that I landed the Pobla de Cabres project. Laurian Thornham also has a house in Spitalfields, although we didn't meet until fairly recently. If you remember, it's her husband who's backing the project.'

When they were nearly there, Diego explained that the one disadvantage of his house was the absence of a garage. He had to keep his car in a nearby lock-up but would drop her and the luggage at the house before putting the car away.

'You don't mind introducing yourself to my housekeeper, do you?' he said, having unlocked his front door and deposited all their baggage in the hall. 'She'll be up on the third floor, watching TV. I'll give her a buzz.' He pressed a button discreetly incorporated in the handsome period door of the tall eighteenth-century house which was his home.

About half a minute later, while he was driving away and Lucinda was looking admiringly at the painted Georgian panelling and the antique chairs, a woman appeared at the head of the first flight of stairs.

'Good evening, Miss Radstone. I'm Muriel Boston.' She came hurrying down to the ground floor; a short plump grey-haired body with kindness and good humour radiating from her pleasant face. 'Are you still feeling poorly? Mr Collingham told me what a dreadful crossing you've had. Never mind: you're at journey's end now, with a nice bath and warm bed waiting.'

'How do you do, Mrs Boston. That sounds lovely. It has been rather a long day,' Lucinda said, shaking hands.

Had she heard correctly? Had the housekeeper said 'Mr Collingham'?

Before she could voice the query, Mrs Boston confirmed that she hadn't misheard her by saying, 'Leave the luggage. Mr Collingham will bring that upstairs. He gets very cross if I carry anything heavy up. "It's bad enough there are so many stairs for you to climb, Mrs Boston," he says to me. As I'm sure you've discovered for yourself, he's a very considerate person . . . not like some men who never notice what's done for them.'

Extremely puzzled by these references to Diego as Mr Collingham, but deciding to wait for him to explain them himself, Lucinda followed her up the wide wooden staircase, its treads showing the wear of many generations of feet.

Half an hour later she was tucked up in bed with a wickerwork tray across her lap and the first mouthful of an omelette, which Paul Bocuse himself couldn't have bettered, proving that Diego had been right in his forecast that she would be hungry by the time they reached London.

He had brought all her luggage upstairs while she was up to her neck in warm water in the attractive bathroom adjoining his visitors' room. It looked now as if she was unlikely to see him again before tomorrow and would have to go to sleep with the mystery of 'Mr Collingham' still unsolved—unless she asked Mrs Boston when she came back for the tray.

One thing Lucinda was sure of now was that Diego definitely hadn't planned to arrive back today. She knew this because Mrs Boston had mentioned that Rosa would be overjoyed, on waking tomorrow, to find that Daddy was back. She missed him when he was away. But as she had already been put to bed, although she was still awake, reading, when he rang up from Dover, he had said she wasn't to be told he was on his way home or she would be too excited to sleep.

As Lucinda was finishing a bowl of fruit salad, there was a tap at the door. 'Come in.'

Expecting to see the housekeeper, she was surprised when Diego entered.

'How are you feeling now?' he asked, leaving the door wide open and coming to stand at the foot of the twin divan in which she was lying.

'Much better, thank you...fine. You must be tired, aren't you? You've driven a long way today.'

'I don't find driving tiring. The journey would have seemed longer had I been on my own.'

The implied compliment made her glow. She wished she was wearing a pretty, feminine nightie instead of a cotton-knit sleep suit, this one with a large banana and an orange printed on the chest. She probably looked about sixteen, which wasn't at all the image she wanted to project.

'Why does Mrs Boston call you Mr Collingham?' she asked.

'I should have explained that earlier.' He sat down on the end of the bed. 'As you know, in Spain a full surname consists of the father's name followed by the mother's. My mother was English by birth—not that one would guess it. When she married my father, she embraced all things Spanish. My full name is quite a mouthful...Diego Cristóbal Alexander Montfalcó Collingham. My maternal grandparents, who never really approved of their daughter marrying a foreigner, insisted on calling me James whenever she brought me to visit them. Later I went to school here, and because my written surname was Montfalcó Collingham I became known as James Collingham in England and Diego Montfalcó in Spain.'

'I think Diego suits you better than James. You don't look half-English.'

'Mama has dark hair and hazel eyes. She might well be Spanish. Rosa also looks Spanish.' The lines of his face seemed to harden. His expression was suddenly bleak. Standing up, he said, 'If you've finished your supper, I'll take away the tray. Have you everything you need?'

'I couldn't be more comfortable...and thank you again for bringing me back with you.'

'It was a pleasure,' he answered, but this time she felt it was a polite rather than a sincere response.

Lifting the tray from her lap, he carried it out to the landing where he placed it on top of a chest while he said, 'Goodnight,' and closed the door.

After a moment or two, Lucinda slipped out of bed to brush her teeth. It had been obvious to her that speaking of his child's Spanish appearance had suddenly reminded him of his English wife. She wondered how long he had lived here...if his wife had also lived here, or if he had moved after she died, unable to go on living in the house they had shared.

All the parts of the house she had seen were furnished in excellent taste and with that extra something which was generally regarded as 'a woman's touch'. But it might be that, since he was an architect, Diego's eye for the finishing touches was superior to that of most heterosexual men; or it might be that he had engaged a professional decorator to organise such things as the basket made of lavender stalks and filled with dried grasses and seed-heads which stood on top of the stencilled chest of drawers between the twin beds. The room was large for a guest room. Lucinda couldn't help wondering whether—if his wife *had* lived here—this had once been the master bedroom.

When she had drawn back the ribbon-patterned green and white curtains at the two multi-paned windows, she climbed into bed and turned out the light. But although she was tired, sleep eluded her. Images of this room, decorated in a different way and with a large double bed in place of the present twins, flashed across her mind's eye.

'Katie...Katie...' Diego had murmured, dreaming of her.

What had Katie been like? Had they slept here? Made love here? How did a young, virile man, long accustomed to the pleasures of the marriage-bed, resign himself to lonely abstinence? For he wasn't the type to seek solace in casual relationships; she felt sure of that. Everything about him—his clothes, his car, his enjoyment of fine food and wine, this beautiful house—were evidence of a discriminating taste, a connoisseur's taste. Such a man would never be satisfied with anything or anyone third-rate. Promiscuous women would have no appeal for him.

Or was she being naïve in seeing him as the epitome of everything she admired in the male sex? No...no, she didn't think so.

'Diego Cristóbal Alexander Montfalcó Collingham,' she whispered aloud. And then, misquoting, '"Once drinking deep of this divinest anguish, how can I face the empty world again?"'

But she knew that although the rough Channel crossing had spared her from saying goodbye to Diego today, she mustn't outstay her welcome. Tomorrow, first thing after breakfast, she must gather her belongings together and get going...out into the empty world.

Because she had opened the curtains the night before, the room was light when Lucinda opened her eyes. For a few seconds she couldn't think where she was. Then she remembered that yesterday she had woken up in a hotel in Lyon and now she was back in London.

The next thing she was aware of was that she wasn't alone...there was someone in the bedroom. As neither Mrs Boston nor Diego would have come in without knocking, her next thought was to wonder if this old house could be haunted. She had never believed in ghosts, but her sense of a presence was so strong that, for an instant, she felt she might have been wrong.

She was lying on her side, facing the windows. Whoever... whatever was there was behind her, in the space between her bed and the bathroom.

Quickly, she rolled over; causing the dark-haired child to jump back with a nervous gap.

As the little girl was about to turn tail and fly to the door, Lucinda said, 'Hello, Rosa. Have you been sent to wake me up?'

Poised to run, the child hesitated. In response to Lucinda's smile, she said, 'I shouldn't have come in— I'm sorry. Daddy will be annoyed with me. But I wanted to see what you were like. He says you were all by yourself in a little house with a palm tree on one side and a fig tree on the other. He made you sound like a white witch... or a fairy,' she said hopefully.

'I'm afraid I'm neither,' said Lucinda. 'But I do have a magic peacock which was left to me by a wise-woman. Would you like to see it?'

'Yes, please.'

'Bring me my bag, will you?' Lucinda pointed it out.

Rosa fetched it and perched expectantly on the side of the bed while Lucinda unzipped the inside pocket containing, in a flat leather case, her grandmother's pendant. Opening the case, she handed it to her visitor.

The child was the image of her father, her dark bronze hair flowing down her back in a straight silky cascade, black eyelashes fringing a pair of large sherry-gold eyes. There was no visible evidence of her accident, but a cosy wool dressing-gown and a pair of knitted slipper-socks hid all but her face and her small delicate hands.

'It's beautiful! Why did the wise-woman give it to you, and how is it magic?'

'Because she loved me,' said Lucinda. 'But the magic is a secret I must never tell anyone until I'm a very old lady and the time comes for me to give the peacock to someone else.'

'Why were you living all by yourself in the cottage?'

'I was only by myself for a short time before your father came. Before that——'

'Before that?' the little girl prompted.

'Before that I was looking after my grandfather while he wrote a book about birds...herons, egrets, wild geese...all kinds of birds. He was almost eighty years old. When he had finished the book he had done everything he wanted to do, so he died. Not long after that I met your father, who offered to drive me to England.'

She had hesitated to explain the reason for her solitude in case, having lost her mother, the child was distressed by any mention of death.

But Rosa's reaction was to say, 'If you hadn't met Daddy before, how did you know it was all right to go with him? Mrs Boston says that if ever I'm out by myself and someone offers me a ride, I must never, never go with them...even if I've seen them before. The only people I may go with are Daddy's closest friends.'

'Mrs Boston's quite right, but it's a little different for a grown-up,' said Lucinda.

She was saved from being asked why by a tap on the door, already some inches ajar.

'Come in.'

Diego put his head round the jamb. 'I thought I told you not to disturb Miss Radstone,' he said to his daughter.

'Rosa didn't. She was just having a mouse-quiet peep at me when I happened to wake up,' Lucinda told him.

'Have you seen her magic peacock, Daddy?' The child crossed the room to show it to him.

'Yes, I have...but she didn't tell *me* it was magic,' he said, with a quizzical glance in the direction of the bed.

'I wasn't sure you believed in magic,' answered Lucinda.

'Of course he does,' Rosa declared. How could you doubt it? her tone said. Leaning against her father, craning up at his face, she said, 'Are you going to be busy today?'

He caressed her cheek with a knuckle. 'Not today. I'm going to spend it with you and Miss Radstone. What shall we do with ourselves? How about a museum, then a pizza lunch, then a movie? If there's one worth seeing.'

She beamed at him. 'That would be super! Do you like museums, Miss Radstone?'

'Very much...but I'm afraid I can't go with you, Rosa. I have a lot to get through today.'

'Oh, dear, what a shame. Can't you really?'

As Lucinda was shaking her head, Diego said to the child, 'Run down and tell Mrs Boston that we're up and about. She can start cooking breakfast.' When she had gone, he said, 'Take today off, Lucinda. Start job-hunting tomorrow.'

'First I have to find somewhere to live...digs or a bedsit.'

'There's no hurry about that. Stay here. Until you've fixed up a job, you don't know what you can afford to spend on accomodation. It makes sense to find a job first, and that might take a week or ten days.'

'I couldn't stay here all that time,' Lucinda protested. 'It wouldn't be right.'

'Don't be silly. Of course you can stay. Why not? I'm not expecting any visitors, so this room will be standing empty. You might as well use it until you can find somewhere decent for yourself. There's no point in moving to crummy lodgings where you won't have anyone to talk to until you start working. Tomorrow night I'm having dinner with the Thornhams. It may be that Laurian will have some useful suggestions about a job and a place for you to live—she has a lot of contacts in London.'

Lucinda's voice was unsteady as she said, 'I—I don't know what to say. You've been so kind to me already. I feel I shouldn't impose——'

'It's settled, then. See you at breakfast.' Diego walked out, closing the door.

She swallowed to clear her tight throat. Her heart felt immeasurably lighter at not having to face the empty world for a little while longer.

'Lucinda's taught me some Catalan,' announced Rosa, when her father came into the first floor sitting-room to find her knitting a scarf for Orson, her bear, and his guest composing a *curriculum vitae* to enclose with job applications.

After yesterday's fun day, as Rosa called it, today had been back to work day for him; and this morning the retired schoolmistress who taught Rosa two days a week, and set work for her to do on the other three, had arrived at ten and left at four.

It was now nearly time for Rosa's supper at six, and this was the first time since breakfast they had seen Diego. All day he had been busy upstairs in what, formerly a silk-weaver's garret, was now his workroom. At lunch time, while the four females in the house had eaten together in the basement breakfast-room, he had had his lunch on a tray at the top of the house.

'Has she indeed? Let's hear it, then,' he invited, sinking into a chair.

Rosa laid down the large wooden knitting needles and drew in a deep breath. In a rapid sing-song, she recited, *'Dotze jutges d'un jutjat menjan fetje d'un penjant.'* It was a Catalan tongue-twister, not unlike 'Peter Piper picked a peck of pickled pepper.'

To Lucinda's pleasure his somewhat weary expression gave place to a delighted grin.

'Well done! D'you know what it means?'

'Twelve judges in one courthouse eating liver from one bunch,' said Rosa, looking pleased with herself.

'She has a very good memory,' Lucinda remarked. 'She picked it up straight away, which is more than I did.'

'Don't tell me you got that out of a textbook,' said Diego.

'No, old Tomás Roig—Maria Roig's father-in-law— taught me to say it when I was starting Catalan and had found that they—that is, you—pronounce 'j' in the English way.'

'Tomorrow Lucinda's going to teach me the days of the week,' said his daughter, a moment before Mrs Boston brought in her supper tray.

'As Mr Collingham's out tonight, I thought I'd watch Terry Wogan before I serve our supper,' the house-keeper said to Lucinda. 'Would you care to come and watch it with me? It's usually very entertaining.'

'Daddy says it's rubbish,' said Rosa, who was only allowed to watch TV with her father's approval, not often given, judging by her very advanced reading skill. She was, if anything, more of a bookworm than Lucinda had been at the same age. And no doubt for the same reason. When a child's life was lacking in some way, as her own had been and Rosa's was now, storybooks offered an escape from painful realities.

Because Rosa had relayed her father's opinion of the programme with no intention of being impertinent, Mrs Boston laughed and said mildly, 'Daddy may not have meant you to repeat his views to other people, my dear.' She smiled at Diego. 'Children! I've no doubt you're right, Mr Collingham. It probably is a lot of rubbish. But you know Wogan's smiling face and his little jokes may not appeal to you, but they mean a lot to some viewers...old people, all on their own, who have no one else to cheer them up.'

'You're quite right, Mrs B. I stand corrected. That reminds me, we're both out tonight.' He turned to Lucinda. 'I should have told you earlier—Laurian rang up today to remind me about her supper party. When I told her about you, she asked me to bring you along. I meant to come downstairs at once, but the telephone rang again and I got caught up in something else. We're bidden for seven forty-five. Is that enough time for you to get yourself ready?'

She had washed her hair the night before, borrowing the dryer Mrs Boston used for Rosa's long hair because her own dryer still had a Spanish plug on it and she was hoping against hope that Diego might yet change his mind and take her with them to Pobla de Cabres.

'It's plenty of time...but how should I dress? Will it be formal or informal?'

'It certainly isn't black tie, but judging by their last party the women will wear evening gear. Not that that's much to go by. I think Laurian herself wore velvet trousers and a sort of sparkly top,' he said, narrowing his eyes in an effort to recall the details of his hostess's appearance.

'In that case I have something suitable,' said Lucinda, rising. 'I'll go up and start on my face.'

'Will you come and show me your dress before you go out?' Rosa called after her.

'I'll come and ask your advice about which earrings to wear,' Lucinda promised.

Fifty minutes later, bathed, her make-up completed, she sat back on the cushioned dressing stool and studied the reflections of herself in the triple mirror.

She had put up her hair, which emphasised her long neck, her only resemblance to her mother. The rest of her features, and her colouring, must come from her father's genes, she thought, looking at her eyes and hoping the way she had done them wasn't too out of date.

The only women's magazine she had seen in Spain, and that not very often, had been *Hola!* a weekly review of the lives of royalty and the jet set. Otherwise she had had to rely on watching how Spanish girls made up to keep her in touch with what was out and what was in.

Before she had gone to Spain she had often wondered if, one day, she would see a man in the street and, finding him strangely familiar, would realise they were alike. In the remote seclusion of the Deltebre she had forgotten those daydreams of meeting her father. Now, back in London, thoughts of him had returned, especially while she was staying in a house where a father and daughter had a particularly close and loving relationship.

Diego had spoken of Rosa having had 'enough traumas' in her short life. At least she still had one parent who was devoted to her. According to her own lights, Georgia had done her duty by her daughter, but she had never loved her as Diego loved his little girl.

Sometimes it hurt Lucinda to see him hug the child, calling her *Rosita mia*—my little rose. Yet at the same time it strengthened her admiration for him, and made her think wistfully that so tender a father must be a wonderful lover.

'I'm sorry to disturb you, Mrs Boston, but would you mind fastening a hook and eye for me, please?' she asked, a short time later, after tapping on the door of the housekeeper's private sitting-room.

'Oh, don't you look nice...all dressed up!' Mrs Boston exclaimed, getting up from a comfortable sofa.

Fortunately, at that moment a pop group was on the TV screen and Lucinda knew the housekeeper wouldn't mind being disturbed while they were on; she had already mentioned that she couldn't abide modern music.

'Thank you.' Lucinda turned round and bent at the knees for the much shorter woman to reach the fastening at the nape of her neck.

'That's a lovely outfit. It suits you,' said Mrs Boston. 'Ah, here's Terry Wogan again. Stay a minute and see what you think of him——' assuming, correctly, that Lucinda hadn't seen him before.

Not being in such a hurry that she couldn't spare a few minutes, Lucinda joined her on the sofa and looked with interest at the man who chaired the most popular chat show on British television.

'...and now, ladies and gentlemen, let me introduce my next guest. The last time she was on the show, I almost got my ears boxed for suggesting that the floodtide of feminism might be on the turn. Here she is...England's answer to Germaine Greer and Gloria Steinem...Ms Georgia Garforth!'

As Wogan pointed an arm towards the far end of the stage, the programme's producer switched to another camera and into the brightly lit studio, to an audience reaction of mingled cheers and boos, walked her mother.

At first Lucinda was too stunned by the unexpected sight of her to take in the preliminary chit-chat as Georgia and Wogan shook hands and she settled herself in the guest's chair and crossed her long, beautiful legs.

Georgia had never been one of the bra-burners; the feminists who felt it was a betrayal of their principles to make up their faces and dress well. It was her declared belief that women must use *all* the weapons at their disposal to fight for the power and authority which, for too long, had been the prerogative of the male sex. No one could ever accuse Georgia of looking drab, dowdy or butch. In fact it was her glamorous appearance which made her one of the most publicised and controversial figures in the women's movement. A lot of non-feminists admired her for her striking looks and quite a number of militant feminists resented and deplored her position as an international spokeswoman.

'Well now, Georgia...sight for sore eyes that you are,' said Wogan, his bright green eyes twinkling. 'What's new in the brave new world of the better half of mankind...pardon me...humankind?'

She laughed, her grey eyes flirtatious. Tonight she was wearing a dress of clinging silk jersey which outlined her curvy figure.

'Well now, Terry, I'll tell you,' she said, with a soft Irish accent instead of her own clipped English voice. She was an excellent mimic, with a flair for making people laugh, as her fans in the audience did now.

But as she was starting to tell him, Mrs Boston used the remote control gadget to switch off the set.

'Did I hear Mr Collingham calling?' she asked Lucinda, who had not closed the door when she came in.

The housekeeper lowered her voice. 'It wouldn't be a good start to your evening out for him to find us watching *her*,' she confided. 'He doesn't think much of the show, but I know he can't *stand* that woman. She's not as bad as some of them, if you ask me. But those feminists are all the same to Mr Collingham. He detests the whole bunch...gets really angry about them.'

At which point Diego looked in to say, 'Sorry to bother you, Mrs B, but I can't find——' He stopped short on seeing Lucinda there.

She stared at him, mentally grappling with the realisation that if Georgia was in London she would have to get in touch with her—without Diego knowing.

Then, as she rose to her feet, everything else was forgotten in the moment of waiting for his reaction to seeing her in the *Laurian* outfit, looking her best.

CHAPTER THREE

'*ESTUPENDO!*' exclaimed Diego, as he took in the lustrous silk-satin shirt and matching but matt silk trousers.

There was an element of teasing in his exclamation, but at the same time Lucinda saw—or thought she saw—the glint of another reaction in the tawny gaze sweeping over her. It was only there for an instant, but it made her heart leap in response.

'What is it you've mislaid, Mr Collingham?' asked his housekeeper.

'What? Oh...only a grey and black handkerchief. It'll turn up, I expect. Not to worry.'

'All your silk hankies should be in the top tray of your wardrobe. I'll come and look. It's possible I've put it in the wrong tray by mistake.'

'What's happened to Wogan?' he asked, noticing the blank screen. 'Isn't he on tonight?'

'Yes, but the guests are a dull lot...not really worth watching.'

The three of them left the room.

The day before, Rosa had taken Lucinda on a tour of the whole house. She knew that Diego slept in a small single room at the far end of the landing, next to the larger bedroom which was now a bed-cum-playroom for his daughter.

Mindful of her promise, Lucinda went to consult Rosa about which earrings to wear. It had been her grandfather's idea that she should have her ears pierced. In Spain, almost from birth baby girls wore tiny earrings.

It made knowing whether to say *'Que guapo!'* of a boy, or *'Que guapa!'* of a girl every much easier.

On their visit to Granada, Constantine Radford had bought her a pair of gold love-knots as a memento of the city. Later, on her twenty-first birthday, he had given her the peacock pendant and also a pair of pearl drops which had been her grandmother's. Last Christmas his present had been another pair of his late wife's earrings, these made from moonstones.

'I like the moonstones best,' said Rosa, after some thought. In her old-fashioned way, she added, 'But really it would look nicest to have earrings to match the peacock's tail.'

'Opal earrings…yes, I think you're right. I shall have to look out for some…when I can afford such extravagances.'

'You're very pretty, aren't you?' Rosa said solemnly, watching Lucinda fix the moonstones in her ears. 'I hope I'll be pretty when I grow up.'

'But of course you will, sweetie. You're pretty already—just like your handsome daddy,' said Lucinda, smiling.

A few minutes later she half-regretted this remark. When Diego came in to say goodnight to the child, Rosa lost no time in reporting that Lucinda had said he was handsome.

He bowed. *'Muchas gracias, señorita.'*

The amusement in his eyes made her blush. Earlier he had been wearing a dark foulard dressing-gown over his shirt and trousers. Now he was in full fig, a plain silk tie and immaculate shirt setting off a superbly-tailored chalk-stripe suit, the missing black-spotted handkerchief overflowing from the breast pocket. Standing there, in the formal array of the well-dressed Englishman, he seemed to her to combine all that was best in both his heritages.

'As it's fine tonight and we're only going a short way, I thought we might walk,' he said. 'Can you walk in those heels?'

'Yes, if you don't mind not striding.'

She had discovered in Lyon that his idea of a stroll was most people's notion of an energetic walk. Being long-legged herself, and wearing low heels on that occasion, she had been able to keep up with him, but only just.

As she rose from the side of the bed and gathered up the other earrings, Rosa reached out both arms for a good night hug. Considering how recently they had met, the child's spontaneous gesture surprised and touched Lucinda.

'Good night, honeybunch. Sleep tight.' She bent to kiss the petal-like cheek offered to her and felt, with a strange inner pang, the soft brush of small lips on her own cheek.

Now I've lost my heart to his child too, she thought, on her way to her room to pick up her bag and a voluminous black wool shawl crocheted for her by Maria Roig.

'Will you be warm enough in that?' Diego asked doubtfully, when she joined him in the sitting-room, the shawl over her arm. He was filling two glasses with sherry.

'Don't you know that women never feel the cold when they're dressed up?' she asked, with a smile. Or at least never when they're also in love with their escort, was her mental rider.

'Laurian tells me that a lot of them now wear a flimsy dress over thermal underwear,' he said, with an answering smile. 'Had that trend begun before you went to

Spain? As far as I know it hasn't reached Barcelona yet. They still seem to be into fur coats there...more so than here, at any rate.'

'New furs were already taboo—or heading that way— when I left. I'm not sure about thermal underwear; I think it was probably still mainly worn by skiers. Do you ski?'

'I used to...I haven't recently. Do you?'

Lucinda shook her head. 'I wish I'd had the opportunity, but I'm told if you're going to be good you have to start about Rosa's age, or even earlier. Shall you teach her?'

'It's not something I've thought about. For a long time after the accident any strenuous activities seemed out of the question.'

'I haven't seen her undressed, but she doesn't seem to be badly scarred.'

'She isn't now, thank God. There are traces, but nothing to make her unhappy and self-conscious. She had the best possible surgeon. I can never adequately repay him for the miracles of skill he performed on her.'

Having started by sipping his drink, suddenly he drained the glass. He said, with a trace of abruptness, 'I think we should be on our way.'

Was he remembering Rosa's mother? Lucinda wondered unhappily. Was that the explanation of the change in his manner—relaxation giving place to tension?

As, quickly, she finished her own drink, Diego picked up the shawl from the chair on which she had cast it. He shook out the folds and placed it lightly round her shoulders.

'Thank you.' Her confidence diminished by the feeling that it was her fault he had been reminded of things he preferred to forget, she picked up her bag and preceded him out of the room.

* * *

'So you've been living in Spain for some time, Miss Radstone?' said Oliver Thornham, the big deeply sun-burned man, rather younger than she had expected, who was the entrepreneur of the Pobla de Cabres project.

Lucinda had been placed beside him at one of four circular tables, each of them seating eight people. Diego was at a different table, as was Thornham's wife, the designer of Lucinda's dress. But whereas Diego had his back to Lucinda, the Thornhams could see each other. Already she had noticed them exchanging glances in a way that, with her intuition sharpened by her own emotional condition, made it instantly clear to Lucinda that these two were deeply in love; moreover, had made love recently, perhaps before dressing for the dinner party.

Whereas with Diego she was always conscious of a deep unrest under a superficial suavity, the man looking down at her now gave off quite different vibrations. She sensed that his life had no flaws, no hidden private tor-ments. Not only was he rich and successful, but clearly his recent marriage to a beautiful talented woman, equally successful in her own career, was above all a love match. They were, without doubt, the two happiest people in the room, and she envied them deeply.

'Only for two years,' she said, in response to his question.

'What do you think of the country?'

'To answer that properly would take me at least ten minutes; but, briefly, I've learned to love it and to want to go back there.'

'I understood from my wife that you were looking for work here?'

'Yes, I am.' She explained the reasons.

'Do you speak good Spanish?' he enquired.

'Yes, and Catalan as well. Also French and a fair bit of German. An ear for languages is my one and only talent.'

'A very useful one, too,' he said. 'You shouldn't have a problem finding an interesting job. If the Pobla de Cabres project were at a more advanced stage, I might have a job for you there. But Collingham thinks it will be a couple of years before we're fully off the ground—by which time, no doubt, you'll be tied up with something else. Collingham has a lot of contacts in Barcelona, I believe. If you want to stay in Spain, couldn't he find a job for you there?'

Lucinda explained that her linguistic skills were more uncommon in England than in other parts of Europe, and that work permits—although gradually being phased out in readiness for when Spain became a full member of the E E C—were still in force.

'Barcelona is full of girls who speak Spain's two main languages fluently and very good English as well,' she said, with a smile.

'Yes, of course...and also Spain's unemployment problem is even more serious than Britain's, Collingham tells me. I was interested to hear that unemployment benefits last for only six months there. Can you explain the system to me more fully?'

Before Lucinda could reply, the man on her other side, who had overheard Thornham's last remark, joined in their conversation by announcing that, in his opinion, everyone receiving benefits from the State should be required to do some unskilled work, such as street cleaning, for the benefit of the taxpayers who were supporting them.

His view was applauded by Thornham, and the two men, finding themselves en rapport, began to discuss all the reforms they would like to see introduced. Neither of them canvassed Lucinda's views which made her smile inwardly, thinking how cross it would have made Georgia to be ignored in this way, even briefly.

The thought of her mother, now somewhere in London and unaware of Constantine's death—not that it would be a grief to her, but she ought to be told—preoccupied Lucinda while her two neighbours expounded their political theories.

How could she contact Georgia? A call to the BBC was unlikely to elicit her whereabouts. Very naturally they would be cagey about giving her address, even to someone who claimed to be her daughter. And if Lucinda gave them her telephone number and asked them to pass it on to Georgia, ten to one it would never be done or, if it were, her mother's call would be answered by Diego.

'This is Georgia Garforth. May I speak to my daughter, please?'

Lucinda could imagine what that would do to her chances, already tenuous, of being taken on as his assistant.

'I'm afraid we're boring you, Miss Radstone. Politics—like the majority of politicians—is a pretty dull subject.'

Underlying Oliver Thornham's smiling apology there was a faint hint of the intelligent male's attitude to the ornamental but not equally intelligent female.

'I wasn't bored,' she said truthfully, not having listened to them. 'Not speaking doesn't necessarily indicate boredom, Mr Thornham. But I've noticed that, on the whole, men prefer to air their views rather than listen to women's. Would you agree?'

He gave her a rather sharp look and she wondered if she had annoyed him. Better that than being written off as a decorative bird-brain.

After a moment, he laughed. 'Yes,' he conceded affably. 'Even those who are married to women of superior intelligence——' he glanced towards his wife '—still tend to assume that pretty women are unlikely to be interested in serious subjects. This is the second time today that I've heard us accused of still doing that. Did you see Wogan this evening?'

'Er...no, I didn't.'

'I don't normally watch it, but this morning one of tonight's guests, Georgia Garforth, rushed into my wife's salon needing something to wear. Naturally Laurian wanted to see how the dress came over on TV, and also she's quite a fan of Ms Garforth's. I like her myself. She's one of the few leading feminists whose opinions impress me.'

It wasn't until much later in the evening, when the delicious meal was over and the guests had adjourned to an upstairs drawing-room—the house had at one time consisted of two flats but was no longer divided, Lucinda had learned during dinner—that she and her hostess were able to talk at greater length than when Diego had introduced them.

With the finesse of a born hostess, Laurian brought another person to join the group having coffee near a splendid eighteenth-century built-in corner cupboard, and at the same time adroitly extracted Lucinda.

'I've seen what you're wearing on quite a number of people, but it's never looked as good as it does on you,' she told her. 'I've been longing for a closer look at that wonderful pendant. Did you find it at Editions Graphiques? I've spent hours browsing over their lovely Art Nouveau things, but I couldn't afford them when I was single. Now Oliver buys them for me. Let's slip upstairs for a few minutes and I'll show you the heavenly thing he found in Paris for my birthday.'

Lucinda strongly suspected that her hostess's real motive in whisking her upstairs was not to show her a jewel but rather, in a most diplomatic way, to give her the once-over.

This house, she discovered when they reached the top floor, also had a silk-weaver's garret, but here it was the master bedroom.

'Do sit down.' Laurian gestured to a sofa before turning away to her dressing-table. 'Before I was married, this room was all blue and white...totally feminine,' she said. 'It had to be made more unisex, and when we went to Bali for our honeymoon I fell in love with the batik sarongs they wear there. I decided to make batik the theme of my next collection and also to redecorate this room with it. I'm rather pleased with the result. It's a better background for Oliver who, as you've seen, is highly macho, but it's also right for me.'

'It's stunning,' said Lucinda, admiring the soft earth colours of the cotton applied to the walls, draped over the huge double bed and used to cover the sofa and a Biedermeier chair. Several patterns had been used, but all were harmonious, reflecting the flair which had made Laurian Thornham a leading designer while still under thirty.

She came to sit beside her guest and show her the birthday present. It was also a pendant: an angel with long golden tresses and *plique à jour* wings, holding aloft a star set with diamonds. The angel's robe, of silvery enamel, was also sprinkled with diamonds.

While Lucinda was admiring it, the older girl said, 'James tells me you're in urgent need of a job and somewhere to live. I might be able to help if you'll tell me something about yourself.'

Although they had only just met, Lucinda felt no constraint about confiding in her. Presently, when Laurian had said that, given a couple of days, she might be able to come up with some suggestions, Lucinda ventured to ask, 'Did you know James's wife?' She found she couldn't get used to referring to him as James when, in her mind and heart, he was entrenched as Diego.

'No, we've only known him quite a short time, and she was killed over two years ago.'

'Killed?' queried Lucinda.

'She was trapped in a fire in a hotel in America. Very few people were burned, but a lot died of smoke inhalation. Poor James...what with that and poor little Rosa being scalded, he's been terribly unlucky in his private life. Career-wise, he's done very well, and of course he's the perfect person to tackle this project for Oliver because of his Spanish connections.'

'Yes,' said Lucinda abstractedly, still shocked by the revelation of how Diego's wife had died. 'How was it that he escaped and she didn't?' she asked, unable to imagine a situation in which he wouldn't either have saved Katie or died in the attempt.

'He wasn't over there with her. If he had been, he'd have got her out—or suffocated with her.' Obviously Laurian's assessment of his character was the same as Lucinda's. 'Although it's completely illogical, I think he still blames himself for *not* being there,' she went on. 'Oliver doubts if he'll ever get over it. But then he and I haven't been married long enough to be able even to contemplate life without each other. People *do* get over tragedies. They have to. Life goes on, and time does heal wounds...eventually.'

Lucinda was silent. It made her feel physically ill to think of what he must have been through after the news came. His adored Katie dead...in dreadful circumstances...on the other side of the Atlantic.

Oliver entered the room. 'Laurian, I realise that you and Miss Radstone have a great deal in common—not least that she looks so charming in one of your designs,' he interpolated gallantly, 'but I don't think this is the time for you two to have a tête-à-tête. Tom Bedworth wants to leave, which he can't without seeing you. He has to operate early tomorrow, and you know how conscientious he is about early nights before a long day in the theatre.'

His wife rose.

'Sorry, darling. I was showing Lucinda the Bricteux angel. I'll come down at once. If you want to check your make-up or anything, the bathroom's through there,' she said to Lucinda.

'I should like to touch up my lipstick.'

'We'll leave you to it and go and do our hostly thing.' Slipping her hand in her husband's, Laurian disappeared.

Did I show what I was feeling? Lucinda wondered, when she was alone. Did she guess I'm in love with Diego?

She remembered Laurian saying that time healed all wounds eventually. Had she once been unhappily in love? Or had it been some other grief which had given that statement the ring of experience?

I like her. She's kind and sensitive and very quick on the uptake. I should like to have her for a friend, she thought.

Presently, crossing the drawing-room landing to return to the party, she could hear the Thornhams' voices and those of their departing guests coming up from the floor below.

For some moments she stood on the threshold of the flower-filled, softly lit room, a little unsure of herself among all these successful people, a little out of her depth.

Then Diego detached himself from a group of four and came to join her. 'Hello. Been powdering your nose? Let me get you a drink. This is a house where the champagne continues to flow until the last guest has departed—usually by taxi.'

'I don't think any more of it ought to flow down my throat. Would a soft drink be possible?'

'Of course... or Perrier, if you'd rather have water?'

'Yes, please, that would be lovely.'

'Have you looked at the portrait of Laurian when she was a child?' Diego pointed out a painting hanging in a shallow alcove with a picture-light casting a gentle radiance over the canvas. 'Oliver calls it "Neptune's Daughter". You can see why.' He went off to fetch the water from a drinks table at the far end of the room.

Lucinda studied the portrait in which Laurian, aged about twelve or thirteen, was sitting at the sea's edge, long hair flowing down her back and her legs hidden by a rock, looking for all the world like a beached mermaid.

'Very nice, don't you think?' said Diego, returning.

'Very. Thank you——' taking the goblet of water. 'You ought to have Rosa done. A pastel perhaps, or one of those red crayon sketches...sanguine, I think it's called.'

'Perhaps I should,' he agreed. 'But I doubt if there's time to arrange it before we leave for Spain.'

'When will that be?'

'I'd like to get down there next month. It depends...'

Partly, she knew, on finding someone to look after Rosa and continue her lessons. A qualified teacher wasn't necessary. With a child of seven, any well-educated adult with a liking for children was capable of teaching her. Lucinda knew she could do it easily, and enjoy it. But it was no use saying so. Diego already knew she was ready and willing. He didn't think she was suitable.

'Laurian feels she may be able to help me get settled,' she told him. 'I don't wonder Oliver fell in love with her. She's very *simpatica*, isn't she?'

'She's one in a million. If she likes you—and she likes most people—she'll be endlessly helpful.'

The man who had sat beside her at dinner brought his wife over to meet Lucinda. With twenty-eight guests still present, not everyone there had met.

Another hour passed before there was a major exodus, leaving the party reduced to ten, including the host and hostess, most of whom lived in Spitalfields and would walk home when they left.

At this stage the party developed into what Laurian laughingly called, 'The dreaded Down Under style—men at one end of the room, women at the other!'

The reason for the segregation was that all the remaining men wanted to hear more details of Oliver's Spanish project, while the women were interested in discussing the fashion scene with one of the Princess of Wales' favourite designers.

It was almost two in the morning when the party finally broke up, with much laughter and joking in the hall as they made their farewells. Some of this small-hours good cheer was a result of the fact that an hour before, sensing that her male guests were peckish again, Laurian had produced crispbreads and an irresistible cheeseboard—even the women had indulged—and her husband had opened the bottles of fine Spanish wine which Diego had brought as a present for him.

Diego's mood, as they said good night, was as cheerful as it had been after dining *chez* Bocuse. Lucinda guessed that there had been a time when he was always like this. Now it took several glasses of wine to deaden his grief, and also his irrational guilt that he hadn't been there with Katie when she had most needed him. He was not tipsy. None of them were—it hadn't been that kind of party. Nor was Oliver the kind of host who would replenish the glass of anyone he suspected of getting near their alcoholic limit.

Nevertheless, had Diego been stone-cold sober, he would not, as they were walking home, have done quite a creditable tap dance up and down a short flight of steps, and then grinned at her and admitted, 'I've always fancied myself in a top hat, white tie and tails, "putting on the Ritz"! What's your secret fantasy, Lucinda?'

Without thinking, she answered at once, 'Dancing a Viennese waltz in a moonlit ballroom in a dress made from acres of tulle.'

'All by yourself?'

This time she did hesitate. 'No... with Rafael Vera, who I think is one of the most handsome men in Europe.'

Diego would know whom she meant. Younger than most important politicians, still in his early forties, Señor Vera was the Spanish Secretary of State.

'He's not here, so make do with me. Let's link fantasies.' Diego bowed from the waist and then held out his arms to her.

It was crazy, but Lucinda didn't care. She went into his arms and felt one encircle her waist and his other hand close over hers. By the night of a nearby street lamp, she smiled up into his eyes and waited for him to start dancing.

But he didn't. His feet stayed still and only his hands moved; the one at her waist drawing her closer and the warm fingers of his left hand tightening round her much smaller right hand.

As they stood there, their shadows merged into one long dark shape on the pavement, she knew he was going to kiss her, and her whole body trembled with longing.

Diego felt it and misunderstood. 'You're cold,' he said, loosening his hold and stepping away. 'You should have said you were freezing.'

'I'm not.'

But it was too late. His impulse was over…gone.

'I thought you'd be cold in that shawl. It's too light for a night like this. Come on: let's hurry.'

Taking her hand, as if she were Rosa's age and inclined to dawdle if not hustled, he began to walk briskly on, forgetting Lucinda's evening shoes and the risk of her twisting an ankle if one of the high slender heels caught in a grating or crack.

Luckily that didn't happen. She arrived at his front door with ankles still in good order, but breathless and bitterly regretful that the chance to be kissed had been lost and might never recur.

When he had unlocked the door and they were in the hall, she murmured, 'Do you think we should have a hot drink? Bovril or something?'

For a moment he seemed to hesitate. Then, also keeping his voice low, he said, 'By all means make one for yourself, if you want to, but I'm going to bed. Mrs Boston will have switched your electric blanket on. I think you'll find that more effective in warming you up than hanging about in the kitchen now that the central heating is off.'

'Yes, I dare say you're right,' Lucinda agreed disappointedly.

They went up the staircase together, Diego dealing with the lights which were all worked by two-way switches.

On the second-floor landing, he bade her a whispered good night. The last she saw of him was a tall silhouette on the threshold of his bedroom in the moment before he closed the door softly behind him.

*　*　*

The problem of finding out where Georgia was staying was solved early the following morning.

Diego took *The Times*, Mrs Boston the *Daily Mail*. Apart from scouring the Sits Vac in Diego's newspaper, Lucinda felt it was important to bring herself up to date with events and trends in England as quickly as possible. There would always be gaps in her knowledge of the past two years here; newsworthy happenings she had missed and might never catch up. For this reason she also read Mrs Boston's paper. In the *Diary* column edited by Nigel Dempster, she found a paragraph about Georgia, for a long time someone he could rely on to do or say something audacious.

> Georgia Garforth, 39 (and holding?), one of feminism's most popular oracles although shunned by the movement's extremists because of her designer clothes and flagrant fraternisation with members of the beastlier half, is in London to promote an updated edition of her best-selling *The Better Half*.
>
> Since it opened, she has stayed at Blakes, the avant-garde hotel owned by Anouska Hempel who also owns Ponds, London's most exclusive dress shop. The sophisticated international atmosphere of Blakes suits Garforth to a T, but this time she isn't accompanied by her long-time handsome French friend Guy Dolancourt, 35.
>
> 'Guy has family problems to attend to. I'll be joining him in Paris when I leave London,' she said, relaxing in the exotic atmosphere of Blakes' famous Chinese room.
>
> But someone who flew from LA to New York recently reports that Garforth and Delancourt, who were also in First Class—she has said that

the battle of the sexes will be over when an equal
number of independent women passengers use
Concorde to cross the Atlantic—didn't speak to
each other between take-off and touch-down.
Which seems a rather long silence if this globe-
trotting couple are, as she claims, as close as ever.

Lucinda left the house early, ostensibly to go job-
hunting. She had already looked up the number of the
hotel in Diego's telephone directory. At the first kiosk
she dialled it.

'May I speak to Ms Garforth, please. This is Lucinda
Radstone.'

After a considerable delay, her mother's distinctive
voice said, 'Georgia here. Where are you speaking from,
Lucinda?' She sounded as if she had been asleep when
the call came.

'London. I saw you on *Wogan* last night. May I come
and see you?'

'I'm terribly tied up today. Why aren't you in Spain?'

'I'm here to deliver Constantine's book to the
publishers.'

'Oh, he's finally finished it.' Georgia didn't enquire
how her father was. 'Well, look, my appointment isn't
till eleven, so you'd better come straight away. It's the
only space in my day and I can be getting ready while
we're talking. How long will it take you to get here?'

'I don't know—I'm not sure where Blakes is. I'm near
Liverpool Street.'

'How dreary! What are you doing there? Never mind:
you can explain when you get here. All the taxi drivers
know where Blakes is. See you soon.' Georgia rang off.

Fortunately Lucinda had enough small change on her
to ring the hotel again and ask which was the nearest
Underground station. A few minutes later she bought a

ticket for South Kensington and braced herself for the remembered ordeal of the Central and Piccadilly lines during the rush hours.

At Holborn she changed to the second line, by which time the crush was easing off and she was able to sit down. She felt tired, having had, at best, only about four hours' sleep. When she had gone to bed, all her emotions had been stirred up by the abortive embrace in the lamplit street.

She had known about desire in theory, but last night had been her first experience of an urgent physical longing for a specific man. Before, although sometimes aroused by a scene in a film or a book, she had never been wildly impatient to find out what making love was like. Many girls of her age had found out, some while still in their teens. Lucinda had always felt it would be better to wait for the man who would be her great love rather than to experiment with boyfriends who were basically just that . . . friends.

Now that she was at last seriously in love, she found that she wanted desperately to feel Diego's lips on her mouth and his hands on her body. Feeling sure that it was a long time since he had made love, she longed to give herself to him and later on, passion spent, to hold him, sleeping, in her arms.

Thinking over the abrupt conclusion of last night's romantic interlude, she wondered if Diego had really misunderstood her shiver. As a man who had once been married, he must know a lot about women's responses. Perhaps he guessed how inexperienced she was and had also recognised her shudder for what it was—a *frisson* of desire.

Perhaps he had drawn away not because he was worried about her being chilled by the night air, but rather for fear that, without meaning to, he might cause her emotions to overheat. To have her falling in love with him might be the last thing he wanted. He wasn't to know that it had already happened; that nothing he did or did not do could change the way she felt about him.

From South Kensington station to the hotel was a brisk fifteen-minute walk. Lucinda hoped Georgia wouldn't be annoyed that she hadn't made the journey by taxi. Even the increase in tube fares had come as a shock to her. What it must cost by taxi she couldn't imagine— and certainly couldn't afford.

Outside the hotel, when she reached it, some expensive suitcases, recognisably Vuitton, were being put into a taxi by a porter. Inside, a feature of the reception area was a stack of Victorian luggage topped by a parakeet's cage.

Presumably warned by one of the girls at the desk that Lucinda was on the way up, Georgia, in a white bathrobe, was waiting at the door of her suite.

'Darling! How nice to see you. It's been a long time. How are you?'

There was nothing insincere in the endearment or in the cheek-kissing motions with which she greeted her child. It was her standard greeting, her standard gesture whenever she met anyone with whom she was on familiar terms.

'I'm well. How are you?'

'Over-worked, under-slept, jet-lagged—but for me that's standard. I'm sorry I can't give you lunch, but I'm booked solid all day. Every journalist in town wants to talk to me. There must be a dearth of celebs this week.'

Fame had never gone to Georgia's head. She knew how little it was worth and took it all in her stride, the bad publicity as well as the good.

'Come through to the bedroom,' she went on. 'Would you like coffee or something?'

'Yes, please.'

Georgia rang room service on the bedside telephone. Arranging her life to avoid spending long in cold climates, she was always becomingly tanned. She had doubtless had a late night and she hadn't yet put on her face, but her looks weren't starting to slip yet. She didn't look young any more, but she still looked extremely attractive.

Now that Lucinda was grown-up, she could see there were certain advantages in having a mother who wasn't possessive, who never fussed or worried, who didn't expect regular letters, who wouldn't insist on organising an elaborate and costly wedding, who would never say, 'After all I've sacrificed for you, I do think you might...' Girls she had known who had suffered from the other kind of mother would have envied her not having to cope with an over-maternal parent.

It would be nice, she thought, watching Georgia on the telephone, if for the first fifteen years one could have a cosy, homely, loving, Mrs Boston kind of mother who would then be miraculously transformed into someone not completely like Georgia but with her best qualities: her tolerance, her sense of humour, her look-ahead attitude to life.

'Where's Guy?' she asked, when Georgia replaced the receiver. She felt slightly guilty at asking when she knew the answer, or part of it. At the same time she was very curious to see how her mother would react when asked about him by someone with whom she didn't have to put up a front.

Georgia moved to the dressing-table and picked up a stretchy bandeau to hold back her hair while she made up. 'We've decided to split,' she said, with a shrug. 'It was beginning to pall. We had a pretty good run...almost five years. At one time I thought it might be a permanent arrangement, but I guess nothing lasts for ever.' She began to dab dots of foundation over her face.

'I'm sorry,' Lucinda said quietly. 'After five years it must be a wrench. I liked Guy...what little I saw of him.'

'So did I...and still do,' said Georgia. 'It was all perfectly amicable. We're still friends...I hope always will be. There was a piece in the *Mail* this morning which implied that we weren't on speaking terms. All rubbish, as most of it is. One of their unofficial stringers reported that we hadn't spoken on a coast-to-coast flight across America. That was true, but it wasn't the whole truth. I was exhausted, as usual, so as we took off I took a sleeping pill and Guy woke me up as we landed at Kennedy.'

'So why the break-up?' asked Lucinda.

'Because he thought we should settle down and try for a baby, would you believe?'

'Really?' said Lucinda, startled.

'No...not really,' Georgia said drily. 'That was the face-saving reason. What he couldn't admit, either to me or himself, was that he could no longer take playing second fiddle in public. It wasn't enough for him that he was the dominant partner in our private relationship; it upset him to read snide comments implying he was some sort of gigolo. Men aren't used to standing back while their wives or girlfriends hog the limelight. It takes an exceptional man—a very secure one—not to mind that.'

'I suppose so.' Lucinda was thinking of Oliver Thornham, so pleased and proud of his wife's success and her fame. But he *was* a very secure man. It wouldn't matter to him how much Laurian was fêted, he would always delight in her achievements, not resent or be jealous of them.

To her own surprise, she said suddenly, 'Do you ever think of my father?'

Georgia gave her a blank look. 'What on earth makes you ask that?'

'*I* think of him sometimes.'

'He's probably dead. He was always risking his neck.'

A knock on the outer door heralded the arrival of Lucinda's coffee. When the interruption was over, Georgia asked, 'How's the old boy?'

'His determination to finish the book kept him going. When it was done, he...gave up. He died about a fortnight ago. That's what I came here to tell you.'

Her mother's hands stilled for a moment, then continued attending to her face. After a pause she asked, 'What are you going to do next?'

'I'm looking for a job in London.'

'Did Constantine leave you anything?'

'A few investments. The income from them isn't much. He didn't leave anything to you, I'm afraid.'

'Why should he? I never liked him—he treated my mother abominably. You only knew him as an old man. When he was young he was utterly selfish and thoughtless...getting her pregnant and then going off on expeditions...never there when she miscarried or when I was born. She put up with it...had no choice; she was financially dependent on him. But as I grew up and saw how put upon she was, I determined never to let it happen to me.'

'Did she complain to you about him?' asked Lucinda.

'Never. She accepted his behaviour as the natural order of things. I didn't. It made me furious.'

'You dumped me on her,' said Lucinda. 'Wasn't that equally selfish?'

'Yes—and don't think I don't know it! But there seemed to be no other option.'

'I should have thought there was one. But you've always stood on the fence on that issue, haven't you?'

Georgia was peering into a magnifying mirror, carefully drawing a flesh-coloured pencil line inside her lower lashes. When she had finished, she sat up. 'I've been a rotten mother by conventional standards, but I wanted to have you,' she explained. 'It's a fantastic experience...having a baby. I wouldn't have missed it. And I didn't dump you on Mother until you were three and out of the messy stage. I did handle the broken nights and the nappies and all that.'

'Yes, Granny told me about that, although I only remember her looking after me. She always defended you when your exploits made Grandfather angry.'

'He was such an old hypocrite. He sowed a few wild oats, you can bet your life on that,' Georgia said cynically. 'Some men of his generation had no scruples at all where women were concerned. Frightfully decent and gentlemanly with each other they were...but absolute swine with women, a lot of them. Have no illusions, my dear. Constantine turned to feathered birds in his old age, but before that...' She rolled her eyes. 'What's his book like? Any good? Did he leave you the copyright?'

'Yes...but I don't know if it's publishable. How many people want to read about the wildlife of the Deltebre? It's a rather esoteric subject, don't you think?'

Georgia nodded. 'But I'm only interested in people. It's no use introducing you to my publisher, he doesn't do that kind of book. But he'll know who does. I can ask him, if you like.'

'Thanks, but Constantine left a list of the firms he wanted me to try it on.'

'Be prepared to wait a long time for them to make up their minds. What's your immediate plan? Where are you staying?'

'I'm putting up with some friends,' Lucinda told her. 'It's only a temporary arrangement. Where are you going from here?'

'First to Australia to do a lecture tour to tie in with the new edition of *The Better Half* and then to explore South-East Asia until the winter is over in Europe and North America. You know I always skip the cold if I can, and I want to see what progress women are making in places like Indonesia. I might just possibly fly back to Europe for Christmas. My publisher has bought himself a ski lodge and he's talking about a house party. It might be fun. But I'll make up my mind nearer the time.'

Georgia paused for a critical look at the colour she had stroked on her eyelids.

'I have several contacts at the Beeb. It's rather late in the day to introduce you as my daughter, but as there's almost no resemblance between us I can pass you off as a friend. Shall I jot down some names?'

'Thanks. They might come in useful, although last night I met Laurian Thornham, the designer, at a party and she thinks she may find something for me. Her husband happened to mention that you'd bought the dress you were wearing on *Wogan* from her. I didn't let on I knew you.'

'Didn't realise she was married,' shrugged Georgia. 'It must have happened fairly recently. She was single when she won the Designer of the Year Award. I remember reading an article about her, and there was no mention of a husband. What's he like?'

'Impressive . . . a good match for her. They look right together.'

'Let's hope it lasts. She's a charmer . . . I've always liked her. She has extensive contacts, so I'm sure she'll put you on to something suitable. Are you all right for money? I can let you have a couple of hundred if that would help?'

'I think I can manage, thanks.'

'How are you fixed for clothes? I've got quite a few discards which I was going to sell off, but you're welcome to any you fancy. Have a look in the wardrobe. They're all on the right-hand side, ready to go to the dealer who buys them from me.'

When Lucinda returned to the house in Spitalfields, she looked as if she had been on an expensive shopping spree. Mrs Boston had lent her a latch-key and she hoped to slip up to her room without anyone seeing the shiny carrier bags with *Ferragamo*, *Chanel* and *Browns* printed on them.

Meeting Rosa on the second flight of stairs, she hoped the child wouldn't pay much attention to the parcels. But although the names on the carriers meant nothing to her, Rosa already knew the difference between ordinary everyday shopping bags and the kind that contained exciting things.

'Have you been buying new dresses? May I come and see?' she asked eagerly.

It was difficult to say no. 'All right, but they aren't things I've bought,' said Lucinda. 'They're what are called hand-me-downs, if you know what that means.'

'I've read about children who never had any new clothes, only things handed down from their elder brothers and sisters. I didn't know it happened to grown-ups.'

'I know someone who has lovely clothes which she only wears a few times. As we're more or less the same size, sometimes she passes a few of them on to me,' Lucinda explained.

In her room she opened the carriers and transferred their contents to hangers. The labels in the clothes weren't the same as those on the bags—the latter had been produced by a chambermaid at Blakes, having been left behind by a departing guest—but they were in the same fashion category. Some of them were American. There was a Geoffrey Beene outfit consisting of a short amber jacket, a dark brown wool skirt and a dramatiic blouse of shot blue-gold silk. There was also a skirt by Ralph Lauren of coppery panné velvet with a toning tweed jacket; sweaters by Missoni and Lotte Gaberle and a slinky acetate-knit halter-neck long body-dress by Azzedine Alaïa which Lucinda wasn't quite certain she would have the courage to put on. Indeed, none of the clothes her mother had given her was right for the life she had left or was likely to lead in the future. The only thing they *were* right for was making a girl in love look her absolutely ravishing best for the man she wanted to love her. It was with Diego in mind that Lucinda had made her selection from Georgia's standards. Whether there would be a chance to wear all these elegant things for him was open to doubt. But she had every intention of making the most of what little time was left to her.

'Daddy's gone into the country to see how the work on a tower he's been having repaired for someone is coming on,' Rosa told her. 'I heard him tell Mrs Boston he'd have dinner on the way back. The tower is a long way away.'

After Rosa had been put to bed, Mrs Boston and Lucinda had supper together.

'There's a lot of fog about this evening, according to the forecast,' said the housekeeper. 'I never like it when I know Mr Collingham has to use one of the motorways and the weather is foggy. There've been so many bad accidents because drivers won't slow down. I'm sure he never drives fast in fog, but other people do.'

Her anxiety was shared by Lucinda, who spent an uneasy evening wondering how tired Diego was after his short night last night, and wishing she hadn't known there was thick fog outside London.

Reluctant to go to bed until she knew he was safe, she sat by the drawing-room fire, determined to stay awake until he came home. But she must have dozed off over the book she had been reading. Suddenly there was the noise of a log being added to the fire and she roused, with a start, to find Diego standing on the hearth rug, looking down at her.

'Oh, you're back!' she exclaimed with relief. 'Did you have a dreadful drive home?'

'It was a bit murky in places. I thought you'd be having an early night after being late to bed last night.'

'I should have done, but——' She changed, 'I was anxious about you' to 'I thought you might come in ravenous and need something hot to restore you.'

'Do I strike you as incapable of cooking a snack for myself?' he asked, crooking an eyebrow.

'Spanish men aren't usually domesticated—or none that I've met.'

'You forget...I'm half-English,' he said. 'The English male is less cosseted. He learns, quite early in life, to make toast and Welsh rarebit . . . bake a potato . . . grill a steak.'

There was a hard note in his voice that Lucinda didn't understand. She felt he was angry with her and didn't know what she had done to deserve his displeasure.

Discouraged from asking him about his day, and if work on the tower was progressing satisfactorily, she said, her manner subdued, 'In that case I'll say good night.'

She was almost at the door when he stopped her in her tracks.

'Would you still like to go to Pobla de Cabres or have you changed your mind since coming back here?'

Lucinda whirled round, her face alight with hope. 'No! Definitely not! Does that mean you've changed yours?'

Diego nodded. 'Yes . . . on the way home.'

'That's wonderful!' she exclaimed joyfully. 'I can't quite believe it. I was so afraid you wouldn't. What made you decide to take me?'

His reply made her wish she hadn't asked.

'Oliver Thornham talked me into it,' said Diego. 'He rang up first thing this morning and said he felt you would be useful when the project gets off the ground. Working for me will keep you on ice, as it were, until he's ready to use you. You seem to have made a very favourable impression on him, and possibly Laurian foresees that you'll also be useful to her. I gather she's planning to spend a good deal of time down there in the future.'

'I see.' Lucinda's delighted expression had faded while he was speaking. 'Is it against your own judgement that you're offering me the job after all?'

He gave her an enigmatic look. 'I wouldn't go as far as that. I've some reservations still, yes. But the Pobla de Cabres project is Oliver's brainchild, and if he sees a future for you there, I'm not going to argue with him. It's late and you look very tired. Go to bed, Lucinda. We'll talk about it in the morning. *Buenos noches!*'

CHAPTER FOUR

'LUCINDA! I can see the Pyrenees!'

Rosa, who had been giving periodic squeaks of excitement ever since they took off, clutched Lucinda's arm and insisted on her craning to catch the first possible glimpse of the snow-covered peaks they would shortly be flying over.

They had the good luck to be travelling on a cold but bright autumn day with no cloud to obscure the patchwork of fields and villages between London and the south coast, the rippled grey silk of the English Channel, the rivers and forests of France and now, in a few minutes, a magician's carpet view of the towering mountains that stretched from the Mediterranean to the Atlantic, forming a natural frontier between France and Spain.

Diego was not flying with them and had missed the amusement and pleasure of watching his daughter's reactions to her first flight. She had loved every second of it: the train ride from Victoria to Gatwick, seeing the X-ray of her flight bag, having her new passport checked, shopping for duty-free presents for her grandparents, waiting to see the gate number of the flight to Barcelona come up on the flicker board and, best of all, the wonder of taking off into a clear sky.

Lucinda, for whom it was also her first experience of flying, was inwardly as excited as Rosa, although rather less thrilled than her small charge by the cunning plastic lunch trays with all their interesting packets and film-wrapped foodstuffs.

'Poor Daddy, missing all this. May I keep that dear little bottle as a souvenir?' the child asked, eyeing the small bottle of red wine which Lucinda had chosen when the drinks trolley paused on its way past.

Diego had gone down by road two days before, his car laden with belongings which it would have been inconvenient to transport by plane. He would be at the airport to meet them. Their first night in Spain was to be spent at his parents' house in the heart of the city.

Rosa wasn't nervous of meeting her grandparents. Apparently, while she was in hospital having her skin grafts, they had flown over to see her, especially her grandmother. But Lucinda was a little apprehensive, having recently found out that Diego's father was the Marqués de Montfalcó y Campassos.

This rather startling information had come from Mrs Boston, who had added that Don Jorge was a kind and most unassuming man but that Doña Julia, though nice, was very particular and could be critical if everything were not just so. Lucinda suspected this of being a discreet understatement on the housekeeper's part and that the truth of the matter was that the English-born Marquesa was all right as long as one kept on the right side of her, but a formidable adversary if one didn't. She hoped she was going to pass muster.

She was as curious as Rosa to see what Spain looked like from the air. The two of them spent the short remainder of the flight peering down at the arid grey-brown landscape, its centres of population far more widely scattered than in England.

The aircraft was Spanish and, when they had landed, Rosa needed no prompting to say thank you and goodbye to the stewardess in their language which was also part of her own heritage.

The passport inspection was slow, causing grumbles even among the Spanish, and then they had another wait until their suitcases appeared. But they weren't delayed going through Customs, and as soon as they emerged into the terminal's main concourse they could see Diego waiting for them. Among the mainly short Spaniards crowding round to greet friends and relations, his tall figure, standing in the background, was immediately identifiable. He was wearing a windcheater of very soft, supple brown leather unzipped over a sweater with a silk scarf tucked inside the crew neck. Although casually dressed, he looked immensely distinguished—every inch an *hidalgo*—and Lucinda's heart turned over at the sight of him.

Leaving her to manoeuvre their luggage trolley through the crowd, Rosa scurried ahead and flung herself into her father's outstretched arms.

When Lucinda joined them he smiled and shook hands, the firm clasp of his long fingers reminding her of the night he had almost kissed her. Her pulses racing, she let him take charge of the trolley and led them outside to the car park while, alongside him, Rosa poured out all the details of their fabulous flight.

The airport was twelve kilometres south of Spain's most important sea-port, but the drive in didn't take long as it was the time of day when shops and businesses were closed and the streets were comparatively empty. The city would come to life again late in the afternoon, Lucinda knew, and would remain busy and lively until late at night. She wondered if there would be a chance to slip out and explore for an hour. She particularly wanted to see the Barrio Gótico, the historic quarter, but perhaps it was nowhere near the house of the *marqueses*.

'*Abuelita* will be resting when we arrive, so you won't see her until later,' Diego said to his daughter who was sitting behind him while Lucinda occupied the front passenger seat. To her, he added, 'My mother has had a *siesta* in the afternoon since she came to Spain as a bride in the fifties. At first you'll find her indistinguishable from Spanish women of her generation, but she still has a core of Englishness which surfaces from time to time.'

'Shall we have to rest too?' asked Rosa. 'Shall I be allowed to stay up late like Spanish children?'

'Tonight you will. At Pobla de Cabres it will be up to Lucinda to decide on the most convenient timetable for you. Did you and your grandfather keep Spanish hours?' he asked, glancing at her.

'We kept birds' hours,' she told him. 'Up early...early to bed. When we went to Granada we had our meals at Spanish times because we were eating in restaurants, but at home we had lunch about noon and supper at seven. At Pobla de Cabres, I think we must wait and see how things go. Obviously *your* timetable will be the governing factor.'

He gave her one of his odd unfathomable looks, but said nothing more.

Lucinda already knew from occasional glimpses through doorways in the towns near the delta that the façades of old Spanish houses often concealed unexpectedly spacious interiors. Sometimes a house with only a metre of pavement between it and the street would have an imposing staircase or an internal garden.

Even so she didn't expect, as they turned down a tree-lined side street in the heart of Barcelona, that a few moments later two great studded gates would open and Diego would swing the car through them into a lofty tunnel leading though to an enormous courtyard. This was surrounded by what looked like stables or coach-houses, with a wide flight of stone stairs leading up to a doorway on a higher level.

'This is the back way in,' he explained. 'The front of the house is on quite a narrow foot-street.'

As he spoke two men, who must have been responsible for opening the gates as soon as they saw his car approaching, came forward to open the car's doors.

'*Buenas tardes. Gracias.*' Lucinda smiled at the old man who was waiting for her to climb out.

He responded politely to her greeting, but he didn't smile. Nor did the other old man when Diego introduced them as Joan and Manolo, two long-serving family retainers. But their faces did break into smiles when he presented his child to them.

'She's the image of you, Don Diego,' said Manolo.

'*Si, es verdad,*' agreed Joan. 'She is the twin of the boy you were at that age...and as mischievous, I shouldn't wonder!'

Beaming, they attended to the luggage. Lucinda had the impression they had reservations about her but were wholeheartedly delighted to see Don Diego's daughter in the house where he had been born and where they had worked since their youth.

It could almost be called a palace, she discovered in the next ten minutes. Never before had she been in a private house of such grandeur as this, except on a visit to an estate owned by the National Trust while she was at school. Even being warned that the Montfalcós were *marqueses* hadn't prepared her for all this magnificence. It was awesome—in more ways than one.

All the public parts of the Casa Montfalcó were furnished with splendid antiques of varying periods, but when they came to the rooms which had been prepared for them—and it was quite a long trek from the courtyard at the rear of the building to the family's part of the great house—Lucinda was relieved to see that, here, modern comforts had been introduced.

She and Rosa had been given a suite; two bedrooms, each with its own bathroom, and a sitting-room in between. This had glazed doors leading on to a small roof-garden amid a landscape of rooftops, most of them covered with traditional Roman tiles, many very old and weathered to wonderful shades of pale coral and faded pink.

'*Abuelita* has made a large garden right at the top of the house. From there you can see the statue of Cristóbal Colon—Christopher Columbus—on his pillar over-looking the port,' Diego told his daughter. To Lucinda he said, 'We are in the Barrio Gótico, the oldest part of Barcelona. When I was small, it's a wonder I didn't break my neck climbing around the roofs! But don't let me catch you trying it, Rosita *mia*, or you'll be in big trouble...*comprendes?*'

Like Lucinda, he was using more and more self-explanatory Spanish words in talking to Rosa, and she was very quick to absorb them.

'The maids will attend to the unpacking,' he went on. 'By the way *castellano* is the language of this household. My father disapproves of the divisive effects of having two languages. At present children in this part of Spain are required to have some classes in Catalan. He thinks it would be more useful for them to be fluent in English, the language of international commerce. I'll go and see if Mama is up yet. If she is, I'll come back for you. It takes visitors a little time to find their own way round this house. It's actually a conglomeration of extensions made at different periods, so it's a bit of a maze.'

'What does conglomeration mean?' asked Rosa, when he had gone.

Lucinda explained, then sent the child to wash her hands and comb her hair. Ought they both to change out of their travelling clothes before meeting the Marquesa? she wondered. How formal was life in this aristocratic *palacio*?

She felt out of her depth and deeply dismayed by the thought that Diego was heir to all this while she was a one-parent child with a mother he disliked and who, no doubt, would be equally unacceptable in his parents' eyes.

Two maids appeared, introducing themselves as Amparo, who was middle-aged, and Nieves, a young girl. Lucinda guessed that she had been named after Nuestra Señora de las Nieves, Our Lady of the Snows, whose statue she had seen in the mountains near Granada.

She asked Amparo if Rosa ought to change before meeting her grandmother.

'Not now, *señorita*, but later, for the party—yes. Show me the child's best dress and I'll press it for her to wear this evening when she meets her aunts and her cousins. Unfortunately Don Mateo and his wife are unable to come—they must attend an important function in Madrid tonight.'

'Who is Don Mateo?' asked Lucinda.

'He is Don Diego's elder brother...Don Jorge's heir,' said Amparo, obviously surprised that Lucinda didn't know this. 'He's in the diplomatic service, as was the Marqués at one time. It was when he was representing Spain in your country that he met Doña Julia, who is English by birth—although one would never think it,' she added, her tone suggesting that this was a very good thing.

At the time Lucinda was too relieved by the news that Diego was a younger son to pay much attention to the maid's manner towards her. Later she realised it had been a mixture of curiosity and veiled hostility. For some reason Amparo was not at all keen on people from England, even though her mistress had her origins there and Rosa's mother had been English.

'*Abuelita* has finished resting and wants to see you straight away,' Diego told Rosa, when he came back. 'You too, Lucinda.'

The Marquesa's quarters were in a different part of the house where the furniture in the corridors, although still antique, was made from light golden woods and looked more French than Spanish.

Diego tapped on one side of a double door. When a voiced called, '*Adelante!*' he opened that half of the door and pushed Rosa gently into the room.

'Darling child! How lovely to see you. Come here and give me a big hug.'

A melodious English voice, full of warmth and welcome, gave Lucinda an encouraging impression before she stepped across the threshold and saw Diego's mother embracing his child.

For a few moments all Doña Julia's attention was focused on Rosa, until she remembered that this treasured little person had a companion and turned to look at Lucinda.

'How do you do, Miss Radstone?' Her left arm still clasping the child, she held out a long thin hand, perfectly manicured and sparkling with beautiful rings. 'My son has told me about you. I've been looking forward to meeting you.'

Her greeting couldn't have been more gracious; and yet, as Lucinda shook hands, she was almost certain she saw, in the depths of the Marquesa's fine eyes, a faint reflection of the look she had seen in the servants' faces. Wariness. Veiled dubiety.

'How do you do?' She could think of nothing else to say. She wanted so much to make a good impression on this woman, but all her poise seemed to have deserted her.

With the ease of an experienced hostess, Doña Julia bridged the awkward moment. 'Do sit down. Tea will be here soon. How was your flight?' she enquired.

Lucinda pulled herself together. 'Extremely interesting for both of us. I hadn't flown before either. We had a spectacular view of the tops of the Pyrenees, didn't we, Rosa?'

From then on it seemed to be all right. Conversation flowed easily among the four of them, and the older woman was so pleasant to her that Lucinda began to feel she must have imagined that she wasn't welcome in this household.

Two more maids had spread a low table with an embroidered cloth and arranged tea things on it, when a manservant came in to say that Señorita Coscollosa had called.

'Show her up, please, Enrico.' Doña Julia turned to her son. 'Sabina has been abroad. I didn't know she was back yet. It will be a nice surprise for her to find you here.' She then turned to her grandchild. 'Our visitor is the sister of Juan Coscollosa who was Daddy's best friend when they were little boys. You will like her. Sabina is great fun and a very good rider. She has represented Spain in show-jumping competitions. If you'd like to, she might teach you to ride. Do you ride, Miss Radstone?'

'I'm afraid not,' answered Lucinda.

'What a pity! It would have been something for you and Rosa to do at Pobla de Cabres. Learning to look after a pony is such good training for children...particularly an only child.'

'Lucinda and Rosa can explore the area on foot,' said Diego. 'Walking is better exercise than riding, in my opinion.'

He rose to his feet as the door opened and a woman in her late twenties came in, her face lighting up at the sight of him.

'Diego! I didn't expect to find you here.' She gave him both hands and tilted her cheek to receive the first of the three kisses exchanged by relations and close friends.

When the introductions were over, Sabina—who was clearly very much at home at the Casa Montfalcó—made her choice from a plate of the sugary Spanish *pasteles* which Lucinda had never much liked, finding them too sweet, and asked, 'For how long are you here, Diego?'

On meeting his child she had switched to fluent if heavily accented English, evidently being aware that Rosa wasn't bilingual.

'Only for one night. Tomorrow the three of us are driving down to Tortosa to stay at the *parador* until the first house at Pobla de Cabres is habitable.'

'Juan comes back on Friday night—he's in Brussels this week. Why not stay for the weekend and drive down on Monday? I know he would like to see you. It's been a long time since the two of you were together.'

'I know, and I'd like to see him, but I can't hang about at the moment. Perhaps another weekend when the project is more advanced,' was Diego's reply.

'We are having a family party this evening, Sabina,' said Doña Julia. 'Won't you join us? You are virtually a member of the family.'

'Thank you, I should like to be present. The party is to celebrate Rosa's arrival, of course.' Sabina smiled at the child. 'Has your father had time to show you the secret door yet?'

Rosa shook her head. 'You didn't tell me there was a secret door, Daddy.'

'When I was a little girl, smaller than you are,' said Sabina, 'my brother and your father locked me in one of the rooms here and told me I'd have to stay there unless I could find the secret door. I searched and searched for it, but I couldn't find it. Eventually one of the servants heard me crying and let me out by the ordinary door.'

'But failed to report their unkindness, or they would have been punished for such unpleasant behaviour,' added Doña Julia.

'I don't think they meant to be unkind,' said Sabina, with a smiling glance at Diego. 'Later on your father said he was sorry and showed me how to open the secret door.'

'Where is it? May I try to find it?' Rosa asked eagerly.

'Yes, Daddy and Sabina will take you while Miss Radstone has a rest after looking after you all day,' said the Marquesa. 'Another cup of tea, Miss Radstone?'

'Thank you.' When the others had left the room, Lucinda asked, 'Does the secret door lead into a secret room? Rosa will love that.'

'Nothing so exciting, I'm afraid. Merely into the corridor. The so-called secret door is a jib-door with *trompe l'oeil* books painted on it so that, at a casual glance, it seems part of the bookcases in one of the smaller *salas*. An adult would quickly recognise it for what it was, but Sabina was only about five when the boys shut her in. No doubt it was Juan's idea. Diego was often naughty in the way of disobeying orders not to do dangerous things, but he was seldom unkind. As they grew up he became very fond of Sabina. At one time we all thought they would become engaged. My husband and I and her parents would have been delighted, but it was not to be.

Diego met Kate and married her almost immediately. Sabina has never married, although she is very popular and, as you see, very attractive.'

Doña Julia handed Lucinda's cup and saucer back to her and changed the subject by asking about Constantine Radstone's book, which her son must have mentioned to her.

Nevertheless she had already made it plain that Sabina Coscollosa was still carrying a torch for Diego and that the Marquesa hoped her patience would not be in vain.

Having taken an instant liking to Sabina, Lucinda could not help sympathising with her for having lost Diego to another girl years ago and for having her hopes revived when he became a widower. She could enter into Sabina's feelings, because she saw every prospect of being in the same boat herself if Diego's youthful affection for the Spanish girl should revive and this time develop into something stronger and more lasting.

'And your parents? Where do they live?' asked Doña Julia presently.

'My mother lives overseas. I—I don't know where my father lives. Unfortunately they separated before...before I knew him.'

The Marquesa looked thoughtfully at her. 'How very sad for you! To grow up with a stable background and the influence of both parents is so much the best start in life, but one which seems less and less common as time goes on. However, here in Spain the family is still a strong unit with less emphasis on careers which take women away from their homes and——'

She broke off as the door opened and they were joined by a tall man with flecks of grey in the thick hair springing from his temples. Although black-haired with dark brown eyes, he was otherwise an older version of Diego.

'Ah, Jorge...just in time for tea. This is Miss Radstone, who brought Rosa from London.'

As the Marqués was in his sixties as well as a man of rank, and she was his son's employee, Lucinda felt she should rise to shake hands with him.

Slightly to her surprise, there was no reserve in his greeting. 'I'm delighted to meet you, Miss Radstone. But need we be formal? My son calls you Lucinda...a charming name. May I use it?'

'Please do,' she said, smiling at him, relieved that he seemed so friendly.

The Marqués sat down on the sofa beside his wife. 'Where are Diego and the child?'

'He and Sabina have taken her to see the "secret" door in the little book-room,' she told him.

'Sabina is here? I didn't realise she was back.'

'Nor did I until she arrived about half an hour ago. She got back late last night, apparently.'

Diego had inherited his trick of hooking up one eyebrow from his father, Lucinda realised, watching lines appear on Don Jorge's forehead as one thick black eyebrow rose at this information.

'She lost no time in calling on you. No doubt she'd heard Diego was back,' he remarked, somewhat drily.

His wife gave him a swift glance which, brief though it was, clearly conveyed a message. But what sort of message it was, Lucinda couldn't tell.

'When the others come back, I wonder if you would mind if I went for a short walk,' she said. 'I've had no exercise today and I should like to have a quick look at the Barrio Gótico while I'm here. I may not have another opportunity.'

'By all means,' said Doña Julia. 'Go now, if you like. You'll need to put on a coat—it's quite chilly today. Do you think you can find your way back to your room?'

'I think so, thank you. Well ... if you'll excuse me ...'

Clearly it was also from the Marqués that Diego had learned his good manners. With the lithe movements of a man whose body is still trim and fit, Don Jorge sprang up to stride to the door and open it for her.

'I understand you speak excellent Spanish and Catalan, so if you should lose your way in the narrow streets of this quarter you'll have no trouble asking for directions,' he said, smiling down at her with a charm which was still very potent in spite of his age.

'None at all. Thank you.' Lucinda left them.

Finding her way to her room presented no problem, but as she put on her raincoat she wondered where the front door was.

She was leaving the room when Diego appeared at the end of the landing. 'I hear you're going for a walk ... if you can find your way out,' he added, with a grin. At that moment he looked so much younger and happier that she felt it must have to do with his reunion with Sabina. 'Let me show you the way, or you may find yourself in the sculleries or even the cellars!'

'*Did* Rosa spot the secret door?' she asked.

'Yes, almost immediately. But she was defeated by the catch which opens it. I was going to show her, but she wouldn't let me. She wants you to try. She feels sure anyone who's had a magical jewel handed down to her must be able to find the way through a secret door.' He slanted another smile at her. 'Perhaps I should give you a clue. I'd like her to keep her belief in magic a little longer.' His expression changed. 'If the good fairy was at her christening, there hasn't been much evidence of it so far, poor scrap.'

Lucinda said quietly, 'But she's well again now. She has you ... whom she adores ... and——' in a lighter tone '—a grandfather who is a marquis and the owner, if not of a castle in Spain, of the next best thing. She'll love coming here as she grows up, and your mother obviously dotes on her. I know from my own experience how important a loving granny can be in a child's life.'

'A loving mother is better.'

It was difficult to tell whether Diego was thinking of the mother Rosa had lost or the stepmother she might have in the future.

While Lucinda was pondering this, he said, in a different voice, 'My father does own a real castle...but it's been falling into ruins for several centuries and what's left is perched on the top of a hill miles from anywhere. When I was a boy I had ambitions to rebuild it. I realised later the impracticability of that idea, but Castell Montfalcó, as it's called on old Catalan maps, was the first signpost to my career.'

'Growing up in this house must also have influenced you, didn't it?'

'To a lesser extent, perhaps. I lived here...took it for granted. When Papa took Mateo and me to see the tumbledown fortress, it fired my imagination. My English grandfather also had an old house which, having no son, he wanted me to inherit when I grew up. That's one of the reasons why I had an English education. My mother didn't want to see her family home sold up because she had been a girl instead of a boy, and with Mateo to follow him here my father agreed to let me be trained to keep Collingham Place going. But it didn't come to anything.'

'What happened?' asked Lucinda.

'My grandfather died too soon...years before I was ready to step into his shoes. The estate was in pretty bad shape and when the finances were worked out it was clearly a hopeless case. My father isn't a rich man— houses like this are more of a liability than an asset, you know—so he couldn't keep Collingham going. It had to be sold after all. A pity, in a way. But it's given Rosa a *dote*, which is good.'

'Do girls still have dowries in Spain?' Lucinda asked in astonishment. 'I thought *dotes* went out years ago.'

'They did—as a condition of marriage. But it never hurts for a girl to have means of her own. Then if she marries a man who can't support her as comfortably as he would like to, she can contribute to their income without having to go out to work.'

'A lot of women like going out to work. They prefer it to domesticity.'

'Then they shouldn't marry,' he said sternly. 'A wife's first duty is to her husband and children. No one can have their cake and eat it. People have to make choices in life. Everyone has to.'

It was clearly a subject on which he had dogmatic views and Lucinda didn't attempt to argue with him, merely wondering if this rather old-fashioned attitude was part of the Spanish side of him.

'Does Señorita Coscollosa have a job?' she asked.

'No, Sabina has plenty to do helping her mother with fund-raising, and training her horses for show-jumping. She leads the life that Spanish girls of good family have always led, but it doesn't mean that she hasn't been usefully occupied. She's learned from her mother how to manage a large house, and how to befriend the lonely and help the sick. "Good works", as they used to be called, still have their place in the world...something else you know from experience. The last years of your grandfather's life were obviously greatly improved by your willingness to go and care for him.'

'Yes...but I wouldn't like to say that I'd have been equally willing had my career been properly launched,' she said honestly. 'It was no great wrench to leave

England just at that point, and I did owe my grandparents more than most granddaughters do.'

They had arrived at the door to another courtyard.
Diego paused before opening it for her. 'I'm sure,
knowing you,' he said, 'that you would never have put
your own interests before his.'

His certainty of her good nature, even if undeserved,
kindled a glow of pleasure.

'Don't think too highly of me,' she said, with a laugh.
'It was a marvellous opportunity to perfect my col-
loquial Spanish and to learn Catalan. I was able to improve my skills and put off joining the rat-race for several
years. Pottering around on the delta was a breeze compared to working in London. I wasn't very attracted by
the nine-to-five, five days a week routine.'

Diego opened the door and they entered the Casa's
front courtyard, which must originally have been open
to the sky but now was glassed over and made into a
huge garden room with a marble floor, raised central
pool and many ferns and indoor trees.

'Perhaps you are like Sabina at heart,' he suggested.
'Perhaps you instinctively know that marriage is the
career for you.'

Sabina. The glow was quenched. 'Perhaps,' she said
non-committally.

'Making this courtyard into an *invernáculo* was my
idea,' he told her, seeing her glance round the place. 'It's
only in July and August that the weather is sweltering.
My parents go into the country then. The rest of the
year, although much warmer than London, Barcelona
isn't too hot. This area is used for parties, saving our
valuable wood floors from being ruined by women's
heels. I'd hoped those thin, damaging heels would go
out for good, but they haven't.'

On the outer side of the courtyard-cum-winter garden was a draughty lobby and a massive door with a wicket in it. Near this was a small room in which sat a small hunchbacked man, evidently the *conserje*. Diego introduced them.

'The key to the large door weighs more than a kilo, doesn't it, Paco?' he said, in Spanish. 'Even the key to the wicket is too heavy to cart around,' he told Lucinda. 'We rely on Paco to let us in and out.'

'Yes, many's the time you and Don Juan have woken me nearer to dawn than midnight,' the porter said, with a chuckle. 'But that was in your youth, and when I was younger myself. The city has changed since then. It's no longer safe to stroll about at the hours you used to come home, Don Diego.'

'You'll alarm the *señorita*, Paco. Barcelona is no more dangerous than any other big city.' Diego turned to Lucinda. 'Would you like me to come with you?'

She would have liked very much to have him as her guide to the old quarter, but she knew it was only politeness which prompted the offer. He would enjoy himself more talking to Sabina, catching up with each other's news.

'Thank you, but I'm perfectly happy to explore on my own. I think you should be with your parents—they don't see much of you.'

'As you wish. I'll see you later, then.' With a nod, he turned away, leaving the misshapen porter to open the wicket for her.

'When you are dressed, *señorita*, the Marquesa would like to see you and the little one in her *tocador*,' said Amparo, having run Lucinda's bath for her. 'Please ring if you need me to fasten your dress, or any other assistance.'

'Thank you, Amparo.'

Unaccustomed to the services of a lady's maid, Lucinda wasn't sure she liked having all her belongings under the supervision of another person. She wondered if Amparo would report to the other maids that the English girl had some good clothes but only cheap chain-store underwear. Lucinda had an idea that Doña Julia, Sabina and Diego's sisters, whom she was going to meet later, would all wear exquisite undergarments handmade by Spanish nuns.

During her walk around the Barrio Gótico she had decided to wear the plainest of her acquisitions from Georgia's wardrobe for dinner tonight. None of the more dramatic things was appropriate to her position here.

Besides, she no longer had any reason to try to glamorise herself. Until today, to entertain the hope that she could make Diego forget his grief for his wife had not been unreasonable. But, now that she knew about Sabina, to try to compete with a girl who had loved him for years, and who was in every way more suitable for him than Lucinda, would be both foolish and selfish. If she truly loved Diego she must put his happiness, and Rosa's, above her own. And there could be no disputing that Sabina was right for him while, in many respects, she herself wasn't.

Attended by Nieves who spoke some English and who had helped her to bath and dress, Rosa presented herself for inspection by Lucinda. She was wearing a dress she hadn't possessed in London; very fine cream-coloured wool with hand-smocking on the chest and at the wrists.

'*Abuelita* bought it as a surprise for me,' she explained. 'I have new shoes as well.' She stuck out a foot shod in a ballet-type slipper of bronze glacé kid. 'Nieves says *Abuelita* asked Daddy to draw round my feet so that she would know my size. I remember him doing it, but he wouldn't say why. Even my socks and my ribbons are new.' She was wearing plain cream knee-length socks and Nieves had dressed her hair with two bows of silk-taffeta ribbon to match the blue silk of the smocking. The effect was slightly old-fashioned compared with the trendy clothes worn by children in England, but it was in keeping with the house and the family who lived there.

'You look very nice,' said Lucinda.

"So do you,' Rosa said politely, not completely hiding the fact that she didn't think plain navy silky jersey, worn with a string of beads instead of the magic pendant, was as nice as the other dresses Lucinda's friend had given her.

They arrived at Doña Julia's boudoir to find her, dressed for the evening in elegant beige crêpe-de-Chine, at work on a piece of canvas embroidery. Having looked approvingly at Rosa, she glanced at Lucinda's dress.

'That looks very much like a Jean Muir,' she said, her tone slightly surprised.

Lucinda agreed that it was.

'Who is Jean Muir?' asked Rosa.

'One of the best British designers. I have some of her things in my cupboards,' answered her grandmother. 'They never date and they pack well.' She put aside her needlework. 'Let's go down, shall we? The others will be here very soon.'

Diego's elder sister, Cristina, had two children in their teens and was now expecting another, due to arrive soon after Christmas. His younger sister, Isabel, had recently had her second child and had not yet recovered her figure. They and their husbands were all perfectly civil to Lucinda but, in spite of their courteous manners, she felt they would have preferred not to have an outsider among them. Even Diego, tonight, seemed somewhat distant in manner. Only the Marqués appeared to

welcome her presence, going out of his way to include
her in the conversation and make her feel at home.

No, perhaps that wasn't quite fair, she thought, when
the party was over and she was back in her room. One
other person there had been noticeably nice to her—
Sabrina Coscollosa.

Why, of all of them, should it be Diego's father and
the girl who loved him who were not guarded with her,
while his mother, sisters and brothers-in-law were
watchful and slightly aloof? What had they got against
her? Something. That much was obvious. But what?

The following day, after breakfast, they set out to drive
to Tortosa, arriving in time for lunch at the government-
owned *parador* on the crest of a hill overlooking the city
and the fertile valley of the Ebro.

By early evening, tired from staying up late last night,
Rosa was becoming drowsy. Lucinda put her to bed in
the room they were sharing, then quietly changed to have
dinner with Diego.

It was difficult not to look forward to a tête-à-tête,
especially as during the day his behaviour had been more
relaxed, reminding her of their long drive through
France, alone together. But these were thoughts she had
to dismiss from her mind. From now on she must try to
regard him only as her employer.

'Did you find my family rather overpowering? There
were moments last night when you looked as if you
wouldn't be sorry to slip away and have some peace and
quiet,' said Diego, after she had joined him in the
spacious bar.

It surprised her to learn that he had taken more than
the most cursory notice of her. She had not been aware
of his scrutiny.

'Not at all. You misread my expression. Last night was a fascinating insight into Spanish family life...and I think most people who aren't part of a large happy family are always rather envious of what they have missed.'

'Among other things a lot of adolescent fights and squabbles,' he replied drily. 'Family life doesn't always run smoothly, you know. When Mateo, Juan and I were at the age to consider ourselves young men of the world, we found the three girls very giggly and silly. I suppose what really annoyed us was that they didn't take us as seriously as we took ourselves then,' he added, with a reminiscent grin.

That rare and charming grin which showed his white teeth and formed little fans of lines at the outer corners of his eyes was always Lucinda's undoing. She leaned forward to pick up the *copita* of sherry which the steward had placed in front of her a few minutes earlier, but her hand was trembling from the force of her innermost feelings and she almost upset the glass.

'Well caught!' said Diego, as she managed to correct the clumsiness without mishap.

The very English comment prompted her to say, 'Did you find that being educated in another country made a gulf between you and the others?'

'Not really. My parents had always insisted that we should grow up completely bilingual. The others—including Sabina—often spent part of the holidays at Collingham, just as I spent a lot of time here. We had the best of both worlds, although for me the emphasis was slightly more English and for them predominantly Spanish.'

'If all of you grew up bilingual, what made you decide not to speak Spanish to Rosa when she began to talk?' This was something which had always puzzled her.

'That was my wife's wish.' Diego spoke of her without any change of expression. 'She had a brilliant brain but no ear for languages. She never understood that small children pick them up very easily. Also Kate didn't like Spain. Well, there are things about this country which can be maddening. The delays...the bureaucratic muddles...the philosophical shrugs when things don't arrive on time. All that she found deeply exasperating. She didn't want Rosa to grow up a hybrid of two cultures but to be totally English. She had very strong views on her upbringing which, at that time, I went along with. I don't think, in the long term, it will be a disadvantage to Rosa. A year from now she'll probably be as fluent as if she had grown up in Spain.'

'I'm sure she will,' Lucinda agreed. 'Did you notice how, on the drive down yesterday, she was reading the slogans on the hoardings aloud to herself? I picked up my first words of Catalan from the notices at the service stations when the coach I was on made coffee-stops.'

He nodded, then turned his head as a couple of foreigners—probably Germans in transit to the south of the country—came into the bar.

Watching his face in profile, Lucinda knew there had been a significant change in his feelings about the past. When she had met him, any reminder of his marriage had caused him pain, even though he had done his best to conceal it. But just now he had referred to Kate in the calm way that people spoke of someone whose memory no longer brings back the anguish of recent loss. There must always be a scar on his heart—how could it be otherwise?—but the wound was no longer an open one. It had healed. She was certain of it—and equally sure what had completed his recovery. It must have been seeing Sabina; knowing all at once that here was someone

he had loved in his youth and now, in maturity, was
ready to love again.

Yet if that were so, how could he have come away so
soon after their reunion? Surely he must have longed to
stay in Barcelona and spend more time with her?

Having exchanged a good evening with the new-
comers, Diego turned back to Lucinda and offered her
the dish of peanuts left by the steward.

'By the way, Sabina is thinking of coming down to
see Pobla de Cabres next weekend,' he told her. 'That
will give you some time off. I can't expect you to be on
duty all day, every day.' Before she could comment, he
went on, 'Tomorrow I'm taking delivery of a Land Rover
which I shall use most of the time, leaving the car at
your disposal. I should think you're quite keen to see
how your place on the delta is faring, aren't you?'

'I'm sure Maria Roig will have been keeping it aired
for me. But I'll take Rosa there one of these days. There
may be some books she would like. I know there's my
grandmother's copy of *The Secret Garden* which I'm
sure she'd enjoy.'

They were the only people in the *parador*'s lofty
dining-room when they went upstairs to dine. Later,
perhaps, some Tortosans might come in, but it wasn't
the time of year for the town to have many foreign
visitors.

'Some of the *paradores* are in castles which have survived largely intact, but this place is nearly all recon-
struction,' said Diego, when they had chosen from the
menu. 'It's the location which makes it. It's a full moon
tonight. After dinner we'll go out and enjoy the view
from the battlements.'

Strolling in the bright moonlight with him was a bitter-
sweet experience. Lucinda had been up to her room to
check that Rosa was sleeping soundly and to fetch a wrap.

The days were still warm, but the night air had an autumnal nip. In England people were already starting to count the remaining shopping days to Christmas. Here in Spain the run-up to the festivities was less long drawn out.

During dinner most of their conversation had been about Pobla de Cabres and some of the previous projects Diego had tackled. Now, as they leaned on a stone wall, looking at the glimmering outlines of the nearby mountains and, below them, the lights of the town, he said, 'You never talk much about yourself, do you, Lucinda? You encourage other people to do it, but you say very little yourself. Sabina remarked on it last night, after you'd taken Rosa upstairs.'

'Did she?' Lucinda wondered if they had all discussed her, debating her suitability for the dual role of Diego's Girl Friday and Rosa's tutor.

'She would like to make friends with you,' he went on. 'Being unmarried at an age when most of her contemporaries are deeply involved in nursery matters, she feels rather out on a limb. Did you like her?'

'Very much. I shouldn't think she'll be single much longer. She seems an awfully nice girl.'

'Sabina's a sweetie,' he said warmly, unaware of the pain he was inflicting.

It was not that Lucinda grudged the other girl her impending happiness; merely that it would have been so wonderful to be Diego's sweetheart herself. But that, in the words of the song, was just an 'impossible dream'.

'Did she say something to you last night that made you suspect she had finally lost her heart to someone?' he asked.

Finally? Didn't he know that Sabina had always been in love with him? How incredibly blind men were!

'No, but she must have a lot of admirers. I should
think any man who fell in love with her would be foolish
to put off telling her,' she answered. 'She's in her late
twenties, isn't she? She must want to start her family
before too much longer.'

'I'm sure she does. She loves children. I don't think
it will be too long before she announces her engagement,' he said, with a smile in his voice that made
Lucinda flinch.

Perhaps it was in his mind to ask Sabina to marry him
when she came down next weekend. Oh, God! How shall
I bear it when they break their news to me? she wondered miserably.

Aloud she said, 'I think I'll turn in now. Good night,
Diego.'

'I'm going to take another turn round the battlements. Good night.'

They parted company.

Next day Lucinda saw Pobla de Cabres—Village of
Goats—for the first time. Approached by a narrow road
which had once been tarmacked but was now full of
potholes and bumps, the village crowned a low hill in
the centre of a mountain-ringed valley. From afar it
looked much the same as any other small place in that
part of Spain. The bell-tower of a church rose about the
Roman-tiled roofs of a tight cluster of houses.

Once they entered the village she saw that, apart from
being deserted, Pobla de Cabres wasn't as typical as she'd
thought. For one thing many of the houses had façades
of undressed stone rather than the more common lime-
washed rendering, and most roofs had a long overhang,
sometimes sheltering a crude timber balcony projecting
from the topmost storey. Her first overall impression was
that here was a place where the winters were very much

harder than down on the delta, and snowfalls not uncommon.

'Yes, when the weather is cold it will be colder up here, but also less broiling in summer,' said Diego, when she voiced her thoughts. 'In general houses in Spain aren't built or equipped to be comfortable during the winter months. A lot of inexperienced villa-buyers get a shock when they find that the marble floors so pleasant to the feet on a summer holiday can make rooms seem like butchers' cold stores during a chilly spell in January. What Oliver Thornham wants here is an almost American standard of winter comfort—but achieving it isn't going to be easy,' he added.

While they were walking around, Lucinda took some photographs of Rosa and also, unbeknown to him, of Diego. It wasn't difficult to pretend to be snapping the architecture of the village while actually taking shots of him as he strode ahead or paused to look at some feature or a façade.

From the top of the village, near the church, came the sound of hammers in use and Catalan voices in loud conversation.

'The workmen putting the finishing touches to our place,' Diego explained.

If only it really was 'our place', Lucinda thought wistfully, as she followed him and his child towards the building where, for a short time at least—how long would depend on how soon Sabina was prepared to get married—the three of them would live together.

On Friday morning, the day before Sabina was due to join them at the *parador*, Lucinda decided to go to the *casita*. But first she drove to San Carlos de la Rápita to buy some gifts for Maria Roig.

It was a lovely day and when they had been to the
market and one or two shops, she took Rosa down to
the harbour. They sat outside the Club Nautico—a
grand-sounding name for a waterfront café used by
workmen and the owners of small boats—drinking Coke
and sharing a dish of *calamares*, which were rings of
squid fried in batter, a bit on the rubbery side but not
bad when eaten in hot sunshine to the tinkle of sailing
boats' stays being plucked by a light breeze.

'It's nice here, isn't it?' said Rosa, happily swinging
her legs. 'Better than London.'

A few days of this golden weather had banished her
northern pallor and bleached the soft tendrils of hair
growing round her high clever forehead.

'Mm...lovely,' Lucinda agreed, closing her eyes and
turning her face up to the brightness. But there was a
dull ache inside her that not even being back in Spain
could ease.

Presently, there being no hurry to move on to the
Deltebre, they went for a walk along the quays. The off-
shore oil rigs were no longer in use, but the town's fishing
fleet was still busy, sending much of what it caught to
the cities.

They were in a part of the harbour where the larger
pleasure boats moored when they put in at San Carlos.
Suddenly, Lucinda had the shock of her life.

Rosa was some yards behind her, having stopped to
re-tie the laces of one of her trainers. So she wasn't a
witness to the moment when Lucinda felt all the
symptoms of breath-stopping, heart-clutching shock.
Nor, had the child been beside her, was it likely she would
have noticed the cause of it.

The cause was nothing extraordinary; only a man on
the deck of an ocean-going yacht calling to someone out
of sight and then another man appearing and the two

of them having a conversation in Spanish. Nothing unusual about that—except to Lucinda, transfixed, momentarily unable to breathe.

One of the men was a Spaniard and the other wasn't. He was stripped to the waist and had a taut muscular torso, but his brown hair was turning grey and his face was that of a man in his middle to late forties. His eyes were his most striking features. They were a clear greenish-grey with a network of fine lines round them.

Lucinda recognised him instantly. She had never seen him before, neither in the flesh nor in a photograph. But she knew, every instinct told her, that this was her father.

CHAPTER FIVE

NOT LONG after Lucinda had sent Rosa downstairs with the message that she was going to lie down because she had a bad headache, there was a tap at the door.

Thinking it must be the chambermaid coming to turn down the beds, she went to the door, intending to tell the girl that she would attend to them herself; even exchanging a few polite platitudes with a maid while she folded back the quilts and the bedclothes was too much of an effort at this moment. All Lucinda wanted was to be alone; to bury her head in the pillow and surrender to the emotions which had been building up, stretching her control to its limit, ever since that shattering moment this morning. The moment when she had looked at a stranger whose face was oddly familiar because, in a masculine form, it bore a striking resemblance to the face she looked at every day in the mirror.

It wasn't the maid who had knocked. It was Diego.

'Rosa says you're not well.'

'It's only a headache. You needn't have bothered to come up.'

To her amazement he pushed the door wider and walked in, forcing her to step back.

'Rosa is worried about you—she says you've looked "funny" all day. She thinks it's more than a headache. If you're not well, Lucinda, tell me. Don't keep it to yourself.'

The kindness in his voice was the last straw. The emotional trauma of the morning, followed by hours of having to hide being upset from Rosa and Maria Roig, had stretched her nerves to snapping point.

'I've told you, it's nothing...a headache...' To her acute dismay, she heard her voice break, felt her mouth starting to tremble, was suddenly in tears.

Trying desperately to control them, she heard the click as the door closed and Diego saying gently, 'Poor girl...' and then, in Spanish, 'Don't cry, *pobrecita*.' The next moment she was in his arms and he was holding her close, letting her weep all over his nice cashmere sweater.

What followed was in one way the most humiliating experience of her life and, in another, the most wonderful.

It was shaming because she had never been out of control before, not even during her childhood when floods of tears were permissible. It was wonderful because, even while she was sobbing and gulping like an hysterical ten-year-old, part of her was aware of the solid wall of Diego's chest under the softness of the cashmere and the strength of the arms which were hugging her.

Like all storms, however violent, it blew itself out eventually. When the brunt of it was over, Diego produced a large handkerchief and put it into the hand with which she was vainly attempting to mop up her streaming cheeks.

'I—I'm terribly sorry,' she muttered, appalled to see the great damp patch on his sweater.

'Don't be. It doesn't matter. Now what was all that about?' he asked, not letting her go when she tried to withdraw from his arms.

Lucinda drew in a long and unsteady breath. One couldn't soak a man's chest and not explain why.

'I...I think I saw my father this morning—he was on a boat in the harbour at San Carlos. I can't be certain

it *was* him . . . but he was very like me. It was just such
an awful shock. It . . . it knocked me sideways.'

And then, because it no longer mattered that her
parents hadn't been married—it couldn't put her beyond
the pale in *his* parents' eyes now that she was out of the
running anyway—she told him everything. Not who her
mother was, but everything else.

'I see,' said Diego, when she had finished explaining.
He kept one arm round her waist while his other hand
came up to stroke back a loose lock of hair which had
fallen across her forehead. 'Yes . . . it must have been a
hell of a shock. If Rosa hadn't been with you, would
you have spoken to him?'

'How could I?' Lucinda answered shakily. 'He doesn't
even know I exist. He may be married . . . probably is.
What would it do to his wife to find out he had a child
by another woman? No . . . no, I could never approach
him. But——' she broke off, shaking her head.

'But you're certain he *is* your father, and you can't
help wanting to know him . . . wanting to have a father,'
said Diego quietly, reading her mind.

She drew another wavering breath. 'I suppose seeing
you and Rosa together has made me even more aware
of all that I've missed, not having one. But I'm not a
child any more. I'm grown-up . . . I don't need a father.
It's better if we never meet . . . if he never finds out about
me. It's even possible I was mistaken about him. The
resemblance between us could have been a coincidence.'

'Perhaps.' He tilted her chin, turning her face up to
his. 'I think you should go to bed. I'll have something
sent up on a tray. There are twin beds in my room too,
so Rosa can sleep with me and leave you in peace. It
wasn't such a good idea for you two to share a room.
It gives you no privacy.'

'I shouldn't have needed privacy if this hadn't happened. I enjoy being——' Lucinda broke off, her heartbeats suddenly quickening.

She looked up. Diego looked down, and all at once it was like that night in the street in Spitalfields, after the Thornhams' party. Only this time it wasn't lamplight. His face wasn't half in shadow. She could see the look in his eyes, feel his arm tightening round her, feel his quickening desire.

What might have happened next was something she would never know. At the precise moment when, for the second time that day, the world seemed to come to a standstill, there came a soft tap at the door, followed by an uncertain little voice calling through the panel, 'Daddy? Daddy... are you in there?'

Diego gave an odd kind of groan and thrust Lucinda away from him. For perhaps fifteen seconds his eyes remained narrowed and brilliant. Then, with a visible effort, he pulled himself together.

He opened the door. 'Hello, pet. What's up?' he asked calmly, holding the door in such a way that Lucinda was still screened from view and had a little more time to recover herself.

Sunrise found her still awake, as she had been for much of the night.

Rosa had not, after all, slept in her father's room. After Lucinda had washed her face and repaired her make-up, she had gone down to join them for dinner. The rest of the evening had passed off in the usual way, with Rosa pleased and relieved that Lucinda seemed back to normal.

But for Lucinda herself, and perhaps for Diego, the normality had been an eggshell-thin crust on the surface of a volcano of unrest. For hours, while Rosa was sleeping, she had lain awake in the silvery gloaming of the moonlight piercing the curtains, trying to fathom what had happened in those moments before the child's hesitant tap had put an end to it.

That what had begun as a comforting cuddle for someone in distress had changed into a potentially passionate embrace wasn't in doubt. The puzzle was...could she have imagined that desirous gleam in his eyes, the pulsing of an urgent need as they stood locked together?

Lucinda knew she hadn't imagined it. For those few moments Diego had wanted her. But he was in love with Sabina. The explanation must be that it was such a long time since he'd held a woman in his arms that contact with a female form—any female form—was enough to arouse his starved senses.

The sun was still low over the distant sea when she slipped out of bed and took her clothes to the bathroom, there to wash and dress without disturbing the dormouse-quiet occupant of the other bed.

Ten minutes later she was tiptoeing along the corridor on her way out for a walk. There were only three other cars, in addition to the BMW and Diego's new Land Rover, parked inside the castellated boundary wall. But the day might bring more than one Barcelona-registered car to the *parador*. The Spanish, she knew, enjoyed going away for weekends, often travelling considerable distances for a change of scene. Sabina was due to arrive in time for lunch, which could mean half past two or three. No doubt she was also awake early this morning— wishing the hours away, longing to be with Diego.

Lucinda walked briskly to the bottom of the hill and then, more slowly, back up it. She was standing near the place where she and Diego had talked on the night they had arrived here, when she heard him say quietly, 'Good morning. You're about early.'

'Good morning.' She gave him a forced smile and resumed her study of the view. 'I like a walk before breakfast.'

'So do I...particularly after a restless night.'

'Didn't you sleep well? Perhaps the moonlight disturbed you. It was very bright.'

He came to stand alongside her. 'It wasn't that. Lucinda——'

Before he could go on, she cut in, 'To be truthful, I didn't sleep very well myself. I couldn't stop thinking about...what happened last night.'

'That was on my mind, too.'

Not looking at him, she said, 'I'd be grateful if you could forget it. I wasn't myself. It isn't at all my style to...to carry on like that. I feel very embarrassed. If we could pretend it never happened—any of it—I'd feel a lot more comfortable.' She gave the words 'any of it' a slight but unmistakable emphasis.

There was a pause. 'Very well...we'll forget it,' said Diego. 'I also wasn't myself. We'll both put it out of our minds. See you later.'

With that he walked briskly away, leaving her torn between relief and regret.

Later, while they were having breakfast, he sent Rosa up to his room for a small black notebook he had left on his bedside table.

When she had left the dining-room, he said, 'About the man you think may be your father...'

Lucinda flushed. 'I thought we'd agreed to forget——' she began.

'Yes, but you won't forget him. He'll always be on your mind.' Before she could deny it, he went on, 'You said he was on a boat with another man who was Spanish. Did you happen to notice the name of the boat?'

She shook her head. 'Only him . . . nothing else.'

'You're quite sure that *before* he appeared you hadn't noticed her name or her port of registration? The mind plays odd tricks. Think hard.'

Lucinda thought back but failed to recall any details. She said, 'I've never been a sailing person; I don't register details of boats. I know it was a sea-going yacht, but where it . . . where *she* came from, I have no idea. What does it matter? If it had been a dull day yesterday we shouldn't have gone to the harbour . . . I shouldn't have seen her . . . or him. It would have been better if I hadn't.'

'Yes, it probably would,' he agreed. 'But as you did see him, it makes sense to try to find out who the man was. You can't do that yourself, but I might be able to. I am—or was—a sailing person. If the boat is still there—which, of course, she may not be—I could wander down there, get into conversation with them, and possibly find out a great deal about the man you saw. I might even find out that he couldn't have been your father because, for example, he was crewing in the Caribbean at the time you were conceived. Isn't it worth trying that to put you out of your uncertainty?'

Lucinda bit her lower lips, torn—as she had been earlier—by conflicting feelings. She couldn't deny that she longed to know more about the man on the boat. At the time she was reluctant to involve Diego in enquiries relating to her irregular parentage.

While struggling to come to a decision, she played absent-mindedly with the salt and pepper containers, first placing them side by side and then one behind the other, a half-conscious indication of what was going on in her mind.

'No, I can't let you waste a morning on such a wild-goose chase,' she said at length. 'It's kind of you to suggest it, but I——'

'My last wild-goose chase in this area was anything but a waste of time,' he interrupted. 'Ask Rosa. With you to take care of her, instead of two elderly women, she's a much happier child.'

'Thank you. I think you're exaggerating, but it's nice of you to say it. But I still can't let you go sleuthing on my account.'

He put his hand over hers, his warm, dry palm resting lightly on the back of her hand, his fingers spreading to her wrist.

'Lucinda, does it embarrass you that your parents weren't married?' he asked her quietly. 'Don't let it. What does it matter? They are the ones who have something to be embarrassed about. They acted irresponsibly.' His well-cut mouth twisted slightly. 'Don't we all, when we're young! But we don't all involve other people in our mistakes. It's no fault of yours if your parents were both rather feckless. You mustn't allow it to worry you. It's clear to anyone who knows you that you haven't inherited their traits. You're thoroughly dependable.'

The touch of his hand, the unexpected encomium, brought a lump to her throat. Deeply moved, but not wanting to show it, she removed her hand from his clasp and sat back in her chair, saying, as lightly as she could manage, 'You're very complimentary today! You make me feel a paragon of all the virtues. I assure you it doesn't bother me...being born out of wedlock. It's not unusual now, is it? Even people who love each other sometimes choose not to make it official now. Here comes Rosa with your notebook.'

The child's return put an end to the conversation, and for the remainder of the meal they discussed other matters.

When breakfast was over, Rosa said, 'We're going shopping for some simple books for me to start reading in Spanish. Will you come with us, Daddy... *Pare*,' she amended, having heard Catalan children addressing their fathers in this way.

'Sorry, I can't this morning. I'm still looking for kitchen tiles. There's a builders' merchant at Aldea where I may find a range I haven't seen elsewhere,' said Diego.

Lucinda had the idea that builders' merchants weren't usually open on Saturdays. Even though Rosa was present, she felt she must say, 'You won't be going anywhere other than Aldea, will you? I—I'd much rather you didn't.'

He gave her one of his unreadable looks. Speaking French, he replied, 'I trust you with my daughter. Can't you trust me?' He stooped to kiss Rosa goodbye. 'See you later, poppet. *'Dios.'* Jingling his car-keys, he left them.

Tortosa was a larger, more affluent town than San Carlos or Amposta. Some of the shops were quite smart and, while she and Rosa were exploring the labyrinth of lesser streets off the main one, Lucinda saw and succumbed to a pair of long leather boots and a fashionable satchel made of the same glossy dark leather. On the salary Diego was paying her she could afford to be extravagant sometimes; and although she no longer had the most exciting of all incentives for looking good, it was still important to keep her morale up. Unhappiness could make people neglect their appearance. She mustn't let that happen to her.

They returned to the *parador* about one o'clock, having arranged to meet Diego in the bar at half past, there to await Sabina's arrival. She could have come down by train because the mainly coastal railway line linking Barcelona with Valencia took a swing inland to include Tortosa among its shops, but she had preferred to travel by car on the *autopista*.

'Did you find the tiles you want, Daddy?' asked Rosa, looking up from a Spanish colouring book when her father joined them in the bar.

'Unfortunately not. I may buzz down to Valencia one day next week—the selection around here leaves a lot to be desired. Have you two ordered drinks?'

'He's bringing ours now,' said Lucinda, as the steward approached with a tray.

Diego asked for a beer and settled himself in a characteristic posture, the ankle of one leg propped on the knee of the other. 'I've already had one beer this morning...outside the Club Nautico at San Carlos.' As she looked sharply at him, he went on, 'They always seem to have at least one fishing boat on the stocks on that piece of land near the Club. I'd like to be there when they launch one. It would be an interesting thing to see.' He paused before adding casually, 'There were no large sailing boats berthed there. The one you saw yesterday had gone.'

She ought to have been annoyed with him for, to some extent, acting against her wishes. Yet she knew that by going to the harbour and finding her father's boat gone, he had saved her from spending the next few days in an agony of indecision; to go back for another look, or not to go back.

Rosa, already made curious by Diego's mysterious remark in French earlier on, now realised that something else not meant for her ears had just passed between the two grown-ups.

'Which boat, Lucinda?' she asked.

But just then Sabina arrived, bursting into the room, her expression radiant.

'Hello...here we are! How are you?'

As Diego rose to his feet, she rushed to embrace him, exchanging the customary kisses with a sisterly vigour quite different from the diffidence or coquetry of most girls kissing a man they loved without knowing what his feelings for them were.

Her 'we' had referred to the man who had followed her in. He wasn't much taller than she was, and inches shorter than Diego. But he was very good-looking in the dark Moorish style of people descended from Spaniards who had intermarried during the centuries of the Moors' conquest of Spain.

He was also very jealous, thought Lucinda, seeing the flash of displeasure in his almost-black eyes as he watched Sabina hugging a personable man of the same age as himself.

Was bringing him here a strategy to make Diego equally jealous? Lucinda wondered. Had Sabina's patience finally run out? Was she determined to know where she stood with Diego? If so, it seemed rather callous treatment of her swarthy escort.

From their admittedly short acquaintance, Lucinda wouldn't have thought the Spanish girl capable of applying the classic opening gambit in a chess game to the management of her love-live. But she didn't really know Sabina, and a girl who had waited ten years for a man to reciprocate her feelings must have reached the point of desperation.

*   *   *

Sabina broke away from Diego and turned to the English girl. 'Lucinda...how nice to see you again.' She kissed her on both cheeks. 'May I introduce my friend Esteban Sanchez?'

'Mucho gusto, señorita.' His greeting was civil, his interest in Lucinda cursory.

'Tanto gusto, señor.'

Sabina completed the introductions. 'And this is my very old friend Diego Montfalcó, whom I've known all my life...and here is his daughter Rosa.'

The ominous glitter dying down when he discovered that Diego, although not displaying the gold band worn by all Spanish husbands, was the father of the child, Esteban shook hands with him.

'What would you like to drink?' asked Diego, beckoning the steward.

Sabina asked for white wine, Esteban for mineral water.

'Esteban is a jockey,' she explained to Lucinda. 'Always he must keep his weight down. He can never eat anything nice or drink any wine, poor thing.'

'There are other pleasures in life,' he said, with a smouldering look which almost made Lucinda laugh.

Sabina giggled.

'What is the joke?' asked Rosa. They had been speaking Spanish.

'Impossible to translate, *preciosa*,' Sabina told her. 'I'm afraid Esteban has no English, or very little,' she added.

'In that case I'd better get on with my colouring,' said Rosa, not a child who expected to be the centre of attention, Lucinda had been glad to find. She began to sharpen a crayon, dropping the shavings carefully into an ashtray.

Her elders made polite conversation until it was decided to go upstairs to the dining-room where a bottle of champagne in an ice bucket was waiting alongside their table.

'Is there something to celebrate, Diego?' Sabina asked. 'Your birthday perhaps?'—to Lucinda, who shook her head.

'I thought you might have something to celebrate,' remarked Diego, as he drew out a chair for Lucinda.

Sabina glanced at Esteban. Then she took a deep breath and said, 'You're right—we are. We are going to be married. You are the first to be told...although you have already guessed.'

'I suspected,' Diego said, with a smile. 'Congratulations, Esteban. You're a lucky chap—this girl is one in a million. Be sure you make her happy.'

'Thank you, Don Diego,' the other man said, as they shook hands again.

'Drop the Don, please...we shall soon be virtually brothers-in-law, as Sabina is like a sister to me. I wish you great happiness,' Diego said to her, repeating the kisses on her cheeks, this time without Esteban glowering.

Then it was Lucinda's turn to offer rather bewildered good wishes, for what *she* had suspected had been so very different from this turn of events. Obviously she had completely misread the situation.

During lunch the whole story came out: how Sabina and Esteban had been in love for a long time but, because he was a jockey, the son of a stable-lad, he was considered ineligible by her parents.

'The fact that he's a *top* jockey and has made—and saved!—a lot of money, and has masses of other good qualities, hasn't changed their minds,' said Sabina. 'But now we've waited three years and very soon I'll be thirty.

So we're not going to wait any longer. If my parents disown me it will hurt me—but not as much as not being Esteban's wife.'

'I'm sure there's no question of their disowning you, Sabi,' said Diego. 'They may be annoyed at first, but I'm sure they'll come round when you make it clear you mean business. It's your mother who's a snob, not your father. Her ideas are behind the times even for Spain.'

'Exactamente!' said Esteban. 'This is what I've been telling Sabina for months past. But she hates to have rows with people...and this will cause a big row...at first.'

While the three of them discussed the situation, and Rosa concentrated on her food and took delighted bird-like sips from the half-glass of champagne which had been poured for her, Lucinda was also silent. She was going over in her mind the effects of her misunderstanding on her relationship with Diego.

If only she had known the truth she would never have implied that she didn't want to remember being in his arms the night before. Nor would she have withdrawn her hand from his at breakfast this morning. He must think now that she disliked his touch, which was the reverse of the truth. But how could she correct the false impression she had given him?

After lunch Sabina and Esteban decided to go for a walk by the river. Diego said he had several telephone calls to make, which seemed rather odd on a Saturday afternoon. Rosa and Lucinda sat outside in the sun, Lucinda reading aloud *The Secret Garden* while Rosa knitted Orson's scarf which was now about two metres long.

That evening, while Rosa had supper on a tray in their room, Lucinda washed and dried her hair and dressed for a celebratory dinner, perhaps to be followed by dancing if they could find a *discoteca* with an acceptable decibel level.

'That's *lovely*,' said Rosa approvingly, when Lucinda had put on a gauzy, lightly beaded dress by Diane Freis which Georgia had bought in Hong Kong.

It was, perhaps, a little over the top for a Spanish provincial town in late November, but Lucinda felt reckless. She had dressed down for the party at the Casa Montfalcó. Tonight she wanted to dress up.

There was no one else in the bar when she arrived there. The barman looked faintly surprised by her sparkly dress but was noticeably more attentive than he had been up to now. She sat on a tall stool and chatted to him, wondering how Diego would react when he saw her.

But the others came down before he did. When he joined them, he appeared not to notice that she had made a special effort. His mood seemed abstracted.

During dinner he talked mainly to Esteban about racing, leaving the women to listen or to start a separate conversation. When the meal was over, he said to Lucinda, 'Unless you particularly want to check out the local discos, I'd just as soon turn in early and leave it to these two to report on Tortosa's nightlife.'

Which left her no choice but to say that she wasn't keen either.

For the second night running, she was awake half the night.

On Sunday they took a picnic lunch to the village and stayed there most of the day. In the evening they drove to a seafood restaurant in San Carlos. Early on Monday morning Sabina and Esteban set out for Barcelona and the confrontation with her parents.

That evening, while Lucinda was alone in the bedroom, the telephone rang and the *parador*'s switchboard operator said, 'Señorita Radstone? I have a call from Londres for you.' A moment later another voice said, 'Lucinda? This is Laurian Thornham. How are you getting on down there?'

'Oh...fine,' said Lucinda, surprised. 'We should be moving to Pobla de Cabres on Wednesday. Is it Diego...I mean James...you want to speak to? Perhaps he's not in his room and they put you through to me. He may still be playing ball with Rosa.'

'No, no—it's you I want to talk to. I thought we might come down for Christmas, bringing some of our friends and making a house-party of it. Except that we'd stay at the Castillo de la Zuda...the *parador* you're in. What I'd like you to do, if you will, is to ask the manager to show you all his nicest bedrooms and to pick out the twelve you like best and reserve them for us. Is that possible?'

'Of course—I can do it tomorrow. When are you planning to arrive?'

'The night before Christmas Eve. We'd fly to Barcelona and then either come down by train or possibly charter a small plane to bring us the rest of the way. Oliver says there's an airfield near San Carlos de Something.'

'There's a heliport—yes. It was used to service the oil rigs when they were working. I don't know how long the runway is, but I expect Diego does.'

'We can check that out later. First I want to be sure there's comfortable accommodation. I'll call you this time tomorrow. How is Rosa taking to Spain?'

'Very happily, so far.'

'And you...are you happy to be back?'

Something in the tone of Laurian's question reminded Lucinda that it had been Oliver Thornham who had more or less forced Diego to bring her.

'Yes, very, thank you,' she said.

They talked for a few more minutes. Then Laurian rang off, leaving Lucinda to marvel at the idea of bringing a party of guests all the way from London to Tortosa to celebrate Christmas. It seemed to her that all these people with whom she found herself mixing—the Thornhams and the Montfalcós—lived at a rarefied level to which she could never aspire. She had more in common with Esteban, although even he had achieved distinction in his sphere. What was special about her? Nothing, she thought forlornly, her spirits at a low ebb.

On Tuesday Diego announced that they wouldn't be moving to Pobla de Cabres the next day because they were going to Barcelona instead.

Concluding that he had some unexpected business there, Lucinda suggested staying at the *casita* until he and Rosa returned, but Diego wouldn't hear of it. She would be needed in Barcelona, he said firmly. Most of her luggage could be left at the *parador*, but she must take something suitable for a drinks party to which they were bidden that evening.

'I can't believe your hosts want me there,' she protested. 'You don't have to include me in all your social engagements.'

'I particularly want you to be there,' said Diego. But not in a tone which made her hopeful that relations between them might improve.

The rift was of her own making; it was she who had rebuffed him. But she felt that to try to explain might only make matters worse. She would have to wait for the right moment to attempt a *rapprochement*.

Having started out early they arrived at the Casa Montfalcó in time to have mid-morning coffee with Doña

Julia. It seemed to Lucinda that this time her manner was friendlier.

'About an hour ago there was a telephone call from London for you, Lucinda,' she said, when the greetings were over. She consulted some notes she had made. 'It was from a Mr John Sidmouth of the publishing house of Sidmouth & Grimston. He tried to contact you at the *parador* first thing this morning, but they told him you were away and gave him our number which you must have left with them, Diego?'

Her son nodded.

'I told Mr Sidmouth you should arrive here about now,' the Marquesa continued, 'and he said he would ring again at noon. I imagine this must have to do with your grandfather's book. Diego told me about it last time you were here.'

'Sounds promising,' said Diego. 'Publishers don't ring up if they're going to turn a book down. He must be interested.'

'Yes . . . how exciting,' said his mother, with the first really warm smile Lucinda had received from her.

Shortly before noon Doña Julia took her to the little book-room with the secret door. 'You can talk to Mr Sidmouth in private here. While you're waiting, see if you can discover the way to open the door,' she said.

In fact Mr Sidmouth's call didn't come through until ten minutes past midday, and it was twenty-five past twelve when Lucinda rejoined the others, her face alight with excitement.

'He *is* interested,' she told them, her eyes at their greenest. 'So much so that he's flying here tomorrow morning to discuss it with me. I hope that's all right, Diego. If you want to get away early, I can go back on the train. Mr Sidmouth has asked me to lunch at the Ritz Hotel. I—I can hardly believe it!'

'That's marvellous...congratulations.' Diego who, with his usual good manners, had risen when she entered the room, took a half-pace towards her but then checked the movement. 'I'm in no hurry to get back. We shall all be agog to hear what he has to say to you. How far did he commit himself on the telephone?'

'I got the impression he was definitely going to publish the book, but with some alterations.'

'How long is he going to be in Barcelona? Is he staying overnight? Perhaps we should offer to put him up?' said Doña Julia, arching her eyebrows in enquiry.

'It's very good of you to suggest it,' said Lucinda gratefully, 'but I gather he's coming for several days—he said something about talks with printers here. I'm sure Grandfather's book can't be his primary reason for coming all this way. He's killing two birds with one stone. Is the Ritz terribly elegant? Will you advise me what to wear, please?'

'Of course, my dear...with pleasure,' the Marquesa responded graciously.

Later Lucinda consulted her about what to wear for the drinks party that evening. Doña Julia came to her room to look at the clothes she had brought with her.

'You have excellent taste,' she remarked. 'And I see that, unlike most girls of your age, you don't fritter your money on a lot of cheap nonsense. You prefer to have a few good things.'

Lucinda could see little point in claiming any credit for her wardrobe. 'Not having earned any money until Diego engaged me, I couldn't afford to buy good clothes or many cheap clothes,' she admitted candidly. 'These were all passed on to me by someone who has money and taste.'

'How fortunate for you.' If the Marquesa would have liked to know who this nameless benefactor was, she was much too well bred to show her curiosity. She advised Lucinda to wear the *Laurian* outfit. 'I expect you'll be invited to dine somewhere afterwards,' she said. 'For lunch with Mr Sidmouth tomorrow this Ralph Lauren coat and skirt will be perfect. The combination of tweed and velvet in this subtle brown is very chic—perfect for the dining-room at the Ritz.'

That evening, when Lucinda was almost ready to go out, greatly to her surprise Diego came to her bedroom.

'Before we go, I must talk to you,' he said, in Spanish. This was because the elderly maid was with her. 'Would you leave us, please, Amparo.'

Her expression disapproving, the maid departed.

'When Amparo was younger it was not done for unmarried girls ever to be alone with men—apart from their fathers and brothers—and certainly not in a bedroom,' Diego said drily. 'Do you find it irritating to have her hovering round you? If so, you must tell her to go away.'

'That would offend her,' said Lucinda. 'I'm getting used to it, actually. What is it you want to talk about?'

Diego put his hands in his pockets and jingled some loose change, his expression oddly troubled.

'You are probably going to be annoyed with me, but please hear me out before you say anything.'

What was all this about? she wondered, turning round on the dressing stool to face him.

'You remember I told you that the boat in San Carlos harbour, on which you had seen a man you thought might be your father, had gone when I went there next day?'

'Yes, I remember.'

'What I didn't tell you was that I made some enquiries. The harbour authorities were able to give me the name of the boat and her Barcelona registration. It was then a very simple matter to find out who was the owner and, through friends who belong to the Yacht Club, something about him and his crew. I now know a good deal about the man you saw. His name is Roderick Tresillian. He's a professional adventurer—in the better sense of the word. He's not married and never has been. I've even been able to find out that six months before your birth date he set out to circumnavigate the world. For the previous six months he was in England, preparing for the voyage.'

Lucinda sat very still. She was remembering Georgia's answer when she had asked her mother if she ever thought of Lucinda's father. *He's probably dead,* she had said. *He was always risking his neck.*

'That's not all,' Diego went on, after a pause. 'Tresillian is still in Barcelona. He's staying with the people whose boat he helped to sail back from Puerto Bañus. He's going to be at the party this evening. Not by chance—I engineered it. In view of what I'd found out, I felt you should have a chance to meet each other.'

The large room was already fairly crowded when they paused on the threshold. There were about fifty people present, all of them holding glasses of champagne and at least half of them talking and performing the graphic gestures which were an essential accompaniment to any Spanish person's conversation.

Nervously, Lucinda scanned the faces of the talkers and the listeners, looking for another foreigner. Perhaps he hadn't arrived yet, or perhaps he was here but screened from her. At the thought of coming face to face, a feeling of panic welled up. She wished she had refused to come.

A palm pressed against the small of her back and propelled her gently forward.

'Chin up!' Diego said softly, close to her ear.

It was such an absurdly British thing to say that, in spite of her intense nervousness, it evoked a slightly hysterical gurgle of laughter.

She looked up at him. 'Please...don't desert me.'

Although she had no language problem, the thought of being left adrift in a roomful of strangers petrified her. Small talk to unknown people was always an effort. Tonight, braced for her meeting with Roderick Tresillian, trotting out suitable platitudes would be impossible.

'Of course not. I'll stay close...don't worry.' He gave her an encouraging smile.

A moment later a woman in black velvet pants detached herself from the throng and came, smiling, to meet them.

'Diego, my dear...how nice...we don't see nearly enough of you.' She offered him her cheeks. 'And this is your English friend...I'm so glad you could come. Let me get you a drink...Juanito.' At her signal a waiter came up and presented a tray of newly-filled tall crystal flutes filled with pale gently-bubbling wine. 'I'm sure you know everyone, Diego. I needn't introduce you. Oh, excuse me...' She moved away to welcome the people behind them.

'I probably do know most of the people here, but first I'll show you the view,' said Diego. He steered her through gaps between the groups towards an array of windows—huge panes of plate glass somehow stuck end to end—overlooking the nightscape of the city.

The apartment was a penthouse at the top of a large modern block somewhere along the Gran Via. An armed security guard was on duty in the ground floor lobby and a liveried porter had checked their names on a list before they were ushered into one of three lifts with large banks of flowers between the doors.

'It's all immensely luxurious, but I like the Casa Montfalcó much better,' murmured Lucinda, as they stood side by side looking down at the lights of Barcelona and its suburbs.

'So I should hope,' said Diego.

Before she could query this rather odd rejoinder, they were joined by a youngish couple who clearly knew Diego well but, like his hostess, had not seen him for some time.

After the introductions, while they were giving him their news, Lucinda's gaze strayed to the rest of the guests. Then, with almost as violent a jolt as when she had first laid eyes on him, she saw Roderick Tresillian.

Tonight he was wearing a well-tailored navy blue blazer, a shirt striped with pink on white and a pink tie. His grey-brown hair was neatly brushed, and his face was strikingly bronzed among the sallow complexions of the Spaniards surrounding him. Was this the man Georgia had once been in love with?

Diego must have spotted him too. Presently, when there was a pause in his friends' conversation, he made a polite excuse to leave them and, taking Lucinda lightly by the elbow, led her away. Her heart beginning to pound, she realised he was going to introduce himself—and her—to the man who might be her father.

'Good evening. I believe we narrowly missed meeting at San Carlos de la Rápita a few days ago—I hear you spent a night there on your way back from Puerto Bañus with Carlos Hernandez.'

'Yes, that's right. You're a friend of his, are you?' the Englishman said, with a friendly smile.

'Diego Montfalcó. How do you do?'

'My name's Tresillian . . . Roderick. How do you do?' Shrewd grey-green eyes studied Diego's face with the close attention of a man whose habit it is to mark and remember the faces of people he meets.

'This is a compatriot of yours...Miss Lucinda Radstone,' said Diego turning to her, his fingers tightening on her elbow.

'How do you do, Miss Radstone.' The other man's greeting was, at first, the courteous reflex of an older man meeting a girl he doesn't expect to interest him greatly. Whatever else he might be, Tresillian wasn't the type to put his hand to his tie and show the lecherous gleam of a middle-aged wolf.

What did show in his eyes, seconds later, was a look of puzzled recognition. He said, 'Did I get that right...Radstone? R for Robert?'

Lucinda nodded, feeling the bones in her hand crunch under the pressure of a grip which doubtless he would have moderated had his mind not been otherwise occupied.

'I used to know someone of that name,' he said, still gripping her hand. 'Constantine Radstone...the explorer. He would be an old man now.'

'He would have been eighty next January, but he died earlier this year. He was my grandfather.'

'Good lord! What an extraordinary coincidence. I knew the old boy quite well...and your grandmother too. I remember her cooking.' Something flickered in his eyes. 'And also your mother, of course.'

Lucinda foresaw, for the first time, a pitfall in front of her. Quickly she turned to Diego. 'Do you think I might have another drink?'

'Of course.' He looked round for one of the circulating waiters but, as there was not one nearby, said, 'I'll go and get one for you. Let me take away that empty glass. What about you, Mr Tresillian?'

'Thank you.' The other man drained his glass and handed it over.

When Diego was out of earshot, she said hurriedly, 'I know this will sound very odd, but would you mind not mentioning my mother's name. I can't explain why at the moment, but it's very important.'

No doubt professional adventurers had to have quick reactions. With scarcely a sign of puzzlement, he said, 'How is your mother? It's many years since I knew her.'

'She's very well. Are you staying here long, Mr Tresillian?'

'My plans are rather fluid. What about you? Are you on holiday?'

'No, I work here...for Señor Montfalcó. He's coming back. Thank you, Diego'—as he gave her a fresh glass of champagne and handed another to the older man.

'Would you excuse me, Lucinda? I've seen a chap over there I want to have a word with.'

'Of course.' She guessed it was an excuse to leave her alone with her father. If he was her father.

'Your employer speaks remarkably good English...no trace of an accent,' remarked Tresillian.

'His mother is English and he went to school in England.'

'Ah, that accounts for it. Shall we find somewhere to sit down? Perhaps it's old age creeping on, but I find these stand-up and shout affairs rather wearing after a bit.'

'We could go outside on to the roof garden. It's quite mild tonight.'

'That's an excellent idea. I'm a non-smoker and whereas in England not many intelligent people are smoking now, here they seem rather less worried about the effects of the habit.'

No one else had ventured outside.

'I'm intrigued,' he said, as they strolled towards the balustrade. 'Why are you keeping your mother's name a secret from Señor Montfalcó?'

'Because he can't stand militant feminists and he might think I shared her views,' Lucinda explained.

'Which you don't.'

'I'm a mild feminist. Georgia is—or was—an extremist. She seems to be mellowing now. How well did you know her?'

'Very well . . . at one time.'

They had come to the railings which were backed and surmounted by netting which didn't obscure the view but effectively prevented the possibility of anyone falling from the garden to the street far below.

'Georgia chose to use her mother's surname,' said Roderick Tresillian. 'You use your grandfather's. Why is that?'

Lucinda swallowed some champagne. 'Because I can't use my father's name. My parents weren't married. I have no idea who he was.'

There was a silence, broken eventually when the man beside her said, 'When were you born?'

She told him.

Roderick Tresillian took off his blazer. 'It's a mild night—certainly by English standards—but shock makes people feel cold.' He draped the coat round her shoulders. 'I think there's a strong possibility that I'm your father, Lucinda.'

When she looked up at him, he added, 'It might be a good idea if we were to have dinner together. We have quite a lot to talk about. Will Montfalcó mind if you desert him?'

*   *   *

The restaurant was small and not busy, although the night was still young. Diego had recommended it when Lucinda had asked him where they could talk in peace.

'...when I finally returned to England, two years later,' Roderick was saying, 'finding Georgia was the first thing I did. Our quarrel had been on my mind all the time I was away. I wanted to make it up with her...ask her, again, to marry me. It was no use. She still felt the same...that I would misuse her in the same way, as she saw it, that her father had misused her mother. I had no idea, no inkling that she'd had a child in my absence. Mrs Radstone gave me no hint of it, when I talked to her. Perhaps Georgia had sworn her to secrecy, or made her believe something bad about me. Your grandfather wasn't there and your grandmother's manner was very constrained, I remember. Hardly surprising, in the circumstances,' he added, with a wry grimace.

The waiter brought the food they had ordered, but neither of them did more than peck at it. They wanted only to talk, to catch up the years they had missed...the whole of Lucinda's lifetime.

When their bottle of wine was empty, and the waiter came to enquire, *'Otra botella, señor?'* Roderick shook his head. 'No, I think not...but we'll have two cups of coffee and I'll have a brandy with mine. What about you, Lucinda?' He had learnt his Spanish in South America, he had told her.

'No, thank you. Only coffee...black for me, please.' After two glasses of champagne and half a bottle of wine, with not much to eat, she was feeling slightly light-headed—or was that merely because this had been such an amazing evening?

'I think I should take you back to wherever you're staying,' her father said presently. 'You're beginning to look rather exhausted. Do you think you can persuade

Montfalcó to give you the day off tomorrow so that we
can spend it together?'

This reminded her of Mr Sidmouth. She explained
about her luncheon engagement.

'As for the rest of the day, I'll have to speak to Diego.
If you'll give me your telephone number, I'll call you in
the morning and let you know. I can't see Diego refusing
to let me have several days off.' She debated telling her
father that all this was Diego's doing, but decided not
to for the time being. 'I'm staying at his parents' house
in the Barrio Gótico,' she explained.

'That's not far from here. Shall we walk? Or are you
wearing high heels?'

Although he had never married, Lucinda doubted if
he had eschewed the company of women. Several things
he had said, including this reference to her shoes, had
given her the impression that the débâcle with Georgia
hadn't made him a misogynist. He was an attractive man
and, although much of his life had been spent far from
civilisation, there must have been periods when he had
been able to enjoy close human relationships.

They walked slowly back to the Casa Montfalcó, filling
in the lost years. They both had so much to tell, but
already there was an instinctive rapport between them.
They were alike in more than looks.

The narrow streets and centuries-old *plazas* of the historic quarter were still full of people when they came to
the Barrio Gótico. In the square in front of the Cathedral
votive candles in crimson casings were on sale, giving a
Christmassy touch to the scene.

'Good heavens! Is this their front door?' exclaimed
her father, when they reached the massive entrance to
the Casa Montfalcó.

'Yes, and the interior is equally baronial,' she told him, as he tugged the great iron bell-pull, causing a muffled clangour within.

Knowing it wouldn't be long before Paco opened the wicket, and uncertain how to say good night or even what to call the man beside her, Lucinda held out her hand. 'Good night...Father.'

He took it, more gently this time. 'I don't deserve that title yet, but I'll do my best to earn it in future. Good night...my dear child. I'll hope to see you tomorrow.' Leaning forward, he gave her the standard Spanish salutation, a light kiss on each cheek.

Then the judas in the wicket opened, an eye peered out, there was the grating sound of a large bolt being withdrawn and, as the wicket itself opened, Roderick walked briskly away.

'Good evening, Paco. Thank you.' Lucinda's voice was husky as she entered the building and spoke to the *conserje*. 'Has Don Diego returned yet, do you know?'

'*Sí, señorita,* Don Diego came in some time back. The *marqueses* are still out—they are at a reception tonight. I think you will find Don Diego in the library, that is where he usually sits in the evening. Do you know the way? Shall I show you? No one else will use this door tonight—I am off duty now.'

'Oh dear...does that mean you've been waiting for me?'

'That is my job, *señorita*. The *marqueses* have given me my own television set to help pass the time, but usually I read. I am a great reader,' Paco told her, with a touch of pride. In Spain, as she knew, there were still many older people whose signature was a cross and who had to have legal documents read to them. 'Come, I'll take you to the library.'

Ten times the size of the little book-room with the secret door, the main library was lit by the flames from a great log of wood burning in the cavernous hearth, and by one green-shaded reading lamp overhanging a deep leather armchair in which Diego's long frame was comfortably sprawled.

'Señorita Radstone, *señor*,' announced Paco.

He withdrew, leaving them alone in the huge book-lined room, the gold-tooled bindings of hundreds of closely-packed volumes glimmering in the firelight, exuding the inimitable fragrance of old leather and hand-made paper.

Diego drew in his long outstretched legs and heaved himself upright. 'How did it go? Did you like him?' he asked.

Lucinda crossed the room to the enormous black fur rug—the skins of several giant bears?—spread in front of the towering stone chimneybreast.

'I think that, already, I love him,' she answered. 'He seems to be everything one could wish one's father to be. It wasn't his fault he didn't know about me. My mother deliberately concealed my existence from him. I—I don't know why.' She couldn't explain Georgia's reasons without revealing her as a radical feminist. 'But I'm sure he loved her and wanted to marry her.'

Diego had changed out of the suit he had worn for the party and was comfortably dressed in old corduroy trousers and a ribbed sweater with suede reinforcements on the shoulders and elbows.

'Don't give your heart to him too quickly, Lucinda,' he said, frowning slightly. 'Don't make a hero of him until you know him better. Life has been pretty tough on you. I shouldn't like to be responsible for causing you any more hurts.'

'My father won't hurt me...I'm sure of that. Oh, Diego, how can I ever thank you for bringing us together? If it hadn't been for you...'

She had already discarded her wrap and her bag, dropping them on a chair on her way to the fireside. Now, on impulse, she moved closer to him and rested her hands on his chest to steady herself as she rose on her toes to press a grateful kiss on his hard cheek.

'Thank you...dear Diego,' she whispered, before her lips brushed his skin.

Then she sank on to her heels, smiling up at him for a moment, intending to step back.

Before she could do so, his arms went round her and he bent his tall head towards her. The next instant his lips were on her mouth and he was kissing her, not with the tentative gentleness of most first kisses but with a flaring of passion like the sudden blaze of a slow fire when paraffin is thrown on it.

If Lucinda hadn't loved him she might have been frightened by the hungry sensuality of his devouring mouth. But this was a moment she had dreamed of—even if never like this—and after two or three seconds she began to respond with all the uninhibited ardour of a girl who was longing to be a woman...Diego's woman.

As he strained her against his strong body she felt, as she had at the *parador*, the throbbing heat of his need; and this time there was no interruption to make him thrust her away from him. Instead he sank down on his knees, taking her with him, until they were thigh to thigh, heart to heart on the rug, her slim arms locked round his neck, his hands searching all the soft curves and flowing lines of her body through the thin silk of her clothes.

Drowning in a whirlpool of emotion, Lucinda flung back her head while his warm mouth explored her throat, feasting on the smooth skin, sending convulsive shudders through her. Lost to everything but the longings aroused by his caresses, she felt him unfastening her shirt, pushing aside the pale satin to expose her quivering breasts in their flimsy lace coverings. Only a small silk bow joined the transparent cups. Groaning, he ripped them apart, pressing his face to her softness, muttering how beautiful she was between more and more passionate kisses.

When he lowered her on to her back, her hair mingling with the dense fur, Lucinda was dimly aware that nothing in her life would transcend the approaching moment when Diego would take her and make her his own. It seemed to her then that a wonderful secret was about to be revealed to her; that, at the moment of discovery, she might die of ecstasy.

Then a branch broke up on the fire, shooting sparks and stirring up wood ash.

It was enough to break the spell. First Diego reared up on his elbows to see if the rug was alight. Then he looked down at Lucinda, naked from throat to waist, her lipstick all kissed away, her eyes bright with desire. Instead of crushing her to him and tearing away the rest of her clothes, which was what she wanted him to do, he suddenly rolled away from her. Then next moment he was on his feet, grasping her hands and pulling her up from the rug.

'I must be out of my mind,' he said harshly. 'Get out of here, Lucinda. Go on, girl... go! While the going's good.'

While she was still too dazed to protest or to grasp what had happened, he hustled her across the room, draped her wrap roughly round her, and bundled her out of the door.

'Go to bed—alone,' were his last words, before he closed and locked it, leaving her, stunned and bewildered, outside in the corridor.

CHAPTER SIX

'Lucinda... time to get up!'

The voice forcing her awake was Doña Julia's. Knowing, while still asleep, that there was some strong reason to resist being woken, Lucinda tried to ignore it. Then came the sudden thought *Rosa*! making her open her eyes and rear up in alarm.

'What's the matter? Is it Rosa?'

'Nothing is the matter. Rosa is out with her father—they've gone to the zoo. Diego left instructions that you weren't to be disturbed, as you were out late last night. But I'm sure you won't wish to rush getting dressed for your lunch with Mr Sidmouth, so I felt I shouldn't let you sleep too long.'

'Oh... I see... no... thank you.' Lucinda rubbed her eyelids which felt dry and inflamed. No wonder: all that crying last night, she realised, memory returning. Could Doña Julia see that she had cried herself to sleep?

The Marquesa had been leaning over the bed, but now had retreated to a chintz-covered armchair.

'In a few minutes your breakfast will be here. Only a very light one, as you'll be eating lunch in less than two hours. Enrico, our driver, will take you to the Ritz. It won't take more than a few minutes to get there. It's on the Gran Via, quite near here.'

'I could walk there,' said Lucinda, wondering why Doña Julia had come to wake her in person rather than deputing Amparo to do it.

161

'No, it's windy today. You don't want your hair blown about. Do you mind if I stay and talk while you have your breakfast?'

'Of course not. But would you excuse me for a moment while I brush my teeth?'

In the bathroom, Lucinda soaked a face cloth in cold water and made a compress for her eyes. She returned to the bedroom to find Amparo plumping up her pillows. When she was back in bed the maid placed a tray across her lap. The breakfast consisted of a tall glass of freshly-squeezed orange juice, a bowl of chopped fruit, also fresh, dressed with yogurt and nuts, and a pot of fragrant coffee.

When the maid had left them, the Marquesa said, 'Diego has told us about your meeting with your father. The name Tresillian rang a bell in Jorge's mind and then he remembered that when he was an attaché at the Spanish Embassy in London he knew someone of that name...Sir Dominic Tresillian, an eccentric Cornish baronet. We've been looking him up in Burke's and it turns out your father is his youngest son. Jorge would like to meet him. I hope you won't mind, when your father rang up a short time ago I asked him to dine with us this evening. Is that all right?'

'It's very kind of you, Doña Julia.'

'Call me Julia, won't you? Doña Julia makes me feel old and rather stuffy...which I'm not when you get to know me. Did you find me a little stiff the first time we met?'

Lucinda took a sip of orange juice. 'I felt you had reservations about me.'

'I did,' the Marquesa admitted. 'My husband thought from the first that you were exactly the right person to have charge of Rosa and be useful to Diego. Jorge's instincts are seldom wrong.' She paused. 'He never liked

Kate...our English daughter-in-law. How much has Diego told you about that unhappy business?'

'Nothing...directly. Someone else told me what happened to her. When I first met Diego, I could see that he hadn't got over it, but lately he's seemed less withdrawn...less haunted by her memory.'

'You felt he was still grieving for her?' the older woman asked.

'Yes, naturally.'

'No, it hasn't been grief which has overshadowed his life,' said his mother. 'If you asked him, I think he would admit now that it was never love Kate inspired...only a reckless consuming physical passion. They were both very young when they married...far too young, we thought. It all came about very quickly, before they really knew each other. They had one happy year together— an extended honeymoon—before they began to realise what they had done: linked two lives which could never mesh. Kate was ambitious, a career girl, a disciple of Georgia Garforth, that tub-thumping feminist who is always inciting women to hate the entire male sex.'

'I don't think she's quite as bad as that,' Lucinda put in.

'Isn't she? I wouldn't know. I only know Diego loathes her...holds her responsible for most of Kate's silliest attitudes. She could have made him a good wife if only she hadn't been obsessed with her career, to the exclusion of everything else. It was because of Kate's career that Rosa was scalded. There was an important meeting Kate felt she couldn't miss. Her usual baby-sitter wasn't available, so she dumped the child with some fool of a woman who put her in a bath with her own five-year-old son and left them alone in the bathroom while she made a telephone call. Rosa was at the taps end. The little boy turned on the hot tap and before the mother rushed back Rosa's whole back and chest had been dowsed with almost boiling water.'

Lucinda gave a soft moan. In her mind she heard the child's screams, felt her agony.

'Diego blamed Kate for putting her job before her responsibility as a mother,' Julia Montfalcó continued sombrely. 'I'm sure she felt dreadful remorse, but instead of showing it, she would round on him. I was witness to some of their rows. We were often in England while Rosa was still very ill. Even then it was Diego who spent the most time at the hospital. I'm afraid the crux of the matter was that Kate hadn't really wanted or planned to have a baby. Eventually they split up...some time before she was killed. There was another man with her on the night she died. Even so, I'm sure it hurt Diego to think of her being trapped. He has a very strong protective instinct towards people weaker than himself.'

Lucinda thought of last night and how he had hustled her out of the library. *Go now...while the going's good.* Had that been his protective instinct at work? Had he guessed she was a virgin who had never experienced passion before?

'It's a sad story,' said his mother. 'But perhaps it may yet turn out well. We hope he'll find someone who'll make him and Rosa happy.'

'Last time I was here I thought you were hoping that Diego and Sabina would marry,' Lucinda ventured.

'Really? Perhaps I mentioned that they were fond of each other in their teens, but it was never more than a boy and girl romance. I gather that you and he were the first to know about this engagement to Esteban Sanchez which has upset Sabina's mother? Diego says he likes him. Did you take to him?'

'Yes...and he must be very much in love to have waited so long for Sabina to stand up to her mother.'

'Griselda Coscollosa is the most formidable type of Spanish matriarch, with some very old-fashioned views,' said Julia. 'But I expect she'll come round in the end. As Shakespeare said, the course of true love never did run smooth.' She rose. 'I'll leave you now. Come and see me before you go out. I'm looking forward to seeing you in that attractive suit.'

So that's the reason nearly everyone here was doubtful about me at first, thought Lucinda, when she was alone. All is explained. Even the staff must know that Diego's marriage to an English girl was a disaster, and naturally that made them dubious about the next English girl to appear on the scene.

Had it not been for her uncertainty about Diego's attitude when next she saw him, Lucinda would have been in a state of unalloyed euphoria as she walked—almost waltzed—back to the Casa Montfalcó from the Ritz.

Lunching there had itself been a memorable experience, but the surprise which John Sidmouth—a debonair man in his sixties with twinkling blue eyes and a great sense of humour—had sprung on her during the main course was so amazing and wonderful that she still couldn't take it in.

After he had opened the wicket for her, it wasn't necessary to ask Paco if he knew where she would find Doña Julia. Lucinda could see from the lobby that the *marqueses* and their younger son were sitting in the far corner of the winter garden.

Both men rose as she walked towards them, but it was on Don Jorge that she fixed her gaze. She felt sure none of them could fail to notice that she was blushing and wondered what the *marqueses* would make of it. Diego—whom she couldn't bring herself to look at yet—would know why the tan she had built up since coming back was now suffused with deep pink. The memory of last night's kisses and her abandoned response to his caresses made it very difficult to hold on to any composure.

'We are all dying to know how you got on,' said Don Jorge, in his idiomatic but slightly accented English. 'Diego is leaving soon, but he didn't want to go without hearing the outcome of your meeting with Mr Sidmouth. Allow me to tell you that you're looking exceptionally charming today. I'm sure Mr Sidmouth must have been pleasantly surprised to find himself lunching with such an attractive young woman. Come and sit down and tell us what *he* was like.'

He indicated the cushioned cane chair next to his. His wife and son were sharing a wickerwork sofa on the other side of a low glass table.

'He was very nice...very informal.' Still avoiding Diego's eyes, Lucinda described the publisher with whom she was already on first-name terms.

'And has he made a firm offer for the book?'

This question came from Diego, forcing her to meet his gaze which incredibly—considering her own inward state—was as calm as if nothing untoward had happened between them.

'Yes, he has.'

Disengaging her glance from that disconcertingly cool sherry-coloured scrutiny, she turned to his mother. 'But not on the terms I expected. He doesn't want to publish the book as a specialised work for serious ornithologists. He thinks it can be made to appeal to a much wider readership. You see, what I didn't know—because my grandfather insisted on parcelling up the typescript himself—was that he enclosed some of my things with it: some poems about the delta and pages from a diary I kept the first year I was there. John—Mr Sidmouth—wants to commission an artist to draw the *casita* and people like old Tomás Roig. He wants the book to be partly my grandfather's text and partly mine. I...I don't know *what* to think!'

'I'm sure Mr Sidmouth knows his business. They are a well-known firm. I often order books published by them,' said Julia. 'Any suggestions he makes to you are sure to be well founded. Did you know Lucinda was a poet, Diego? You never told me.'

'She has never mentioned it,' he answered.

'I'm not really a poet,' said Lucinda. 'It's only blank verse, it doesn't rhyme. I write it for my own amusement.'

'It must be exceptionally good blank verse to be publishable,' remarked Don Jorge. 'It seems you have other talents to add to your gift for languages. I must say I think you are being wasted on this work for my son at Pobla de Cabres.'

His expression and his tone made it clear that he didn't intend this remark to be taken literally. It was meant as a jocular compliment.

Both he and his wife looked startled when Diego said, 'Very true. I had already been coming to that conclusion before this development. I've been reconsidering your view that Rosa ought to start mixing with other children, Mama. I believe you're right. Instead of taking her back to Tortosa with me, I propose now to leave her here. Lucinda can continue to teach her until she has learnt enough Spanish to start school, but, with other people to share the responsibility, she'll have enough time to do what her publisher requires of her. I shall drive, or fly up at weekends. That will be an altogether better arrangement than the original plan.'

Lucinda was momentarily too dumbfounded to utter.

His mother said, 'I agree—much more sensible. It's exactly what I had in mind, but I didn't urge it upon you because one is always reluctant to seem interfering. Don't you think it's a better plan, Jorge?'

'It would certainly allow Lucinda more time to work on her book, but she may not be keen on living in the centre of a city,' the Marqués suggested, smiling at her. 'I think you prefer the country, don't you, Lucinda?'

Something in his wise dark eyes made her suspect that he knew all that mattered to her was to be near Diego.

'Yes, I do,' she agreed. 'And *I* think a country life is better for children unless they must live in a city.' She turned to the Marquesa. 'I don't want to disagree with you, but Rosa *needs* the outdoor life at Pobla de Cabres. Just in the short time we've been at Tortosa, she's begun to look a different child. Until she has mastered enough Spanish to attend school, I feel she should be with her father...whom she adores. No one can take his place in her life'—nor in mine!—'not even loving grandparents. I'm sure her transition from England to Spain will be accomplished more smoothly if she spends the winter at the village with plenty of fresh air and as much sun as possible, and Diego there every day, not only at weekends.'

It was, for her, quite a speech, and expressed with a force and conviction which clearly surprised the two older people, and even Lucinda herself.

As was so often the case, Diego's reaction was masked by an expression of total inscrutability.

In case she had sounded too forceful, she went on more gently, 'I hope you don't mind my saying what I think, but I'm very attached to Rosa and I think I understand her...having been an only child myself.'

'She is obviously very attached to you, my dear,' said Don Jorge. 'I do feel, Julia, that our view of the situation may be colored by our desire to have the amusement and pleasure of the child's presence in the house. She's a most diverting little thing.'

'Perhaps you're right,' said his wife, rather reluctantly. 'I must admit I do love having her here. At the same time I can't deny that the air of Pobla de Cabres must be healthier for her than our fume-filled city atmosphere—although, being on the Mediterranean, I don't think Barcelona is as unhealthy as London or Madrid.'

'Nevertheless she is staying here.' Diego's tone brooked no further discussion. 'I must be off. I'm sorry to miss meeting your father properly at dinner tonight, Lucinda, but no doubt he'll still be around when I come back next weekend. Goodbye, Mama.'

He embraced his mother and shook hands with his father, but also kissed him on both cheeks in the affectionate way which was customary in Spain when fathers and sons met or parted. It was a facet of Spanish family life which, normally, Lucinda found rather touching, but at the moment she had other things on her mind.

Already on her feet when Diego turned to shake hands with her, she said, 'Before you leave, may I speak to you in private, please?' And the spark in her eyes and the lift of her chin made it clear to him that he had better consent or she would say what she must in front of his parents.

'You two stay here. We'll go and find Rosa,' said the Marquesa. 'Now that she's discovered the kitchens and made friends with Jefe Gilabert——' this was the Montfalcós' chef or *jefe de cocina* '—I expect we shall have to retrieve her from his domain quite often, as we did when our children were her age. We had another chef then.'

Apparently unaware of any undercurrents, she led her husband away.

As soon as they were out of earshot, Lucinda said, 'This time yesterday you hadn't decided to leave Rosa here. I think it's because of...of what happened last night.' Her blush revived, tinging her suntan even more deeply than before, but her gaze didn't waver. Her eyes met his squarely and steadily.

She thought Diego might deny that last night had anything to do with today's decision.

Slightly to her surprise, he agreed, 'It has a lot to do with it—yes. Last night proved to me, and I should have thought to you also, that for us to live at Pobla de Cabres, in the same house, with no one else around, is not on. If you want me to spell it out for you, I can't rely on myself not to make another pass at you. I'm aware that you didn't intend to be...provocative last night. You don't have to tell me that. What you obviously don't understand is that I have a low boiling point. To put it bluntly, it's been a long time since I made love to a woman...and you are a very lovely girl. I'm not going to apologise for what happened, but I'm going to make sure it doesn't happen again.'

Lucinda didn't speak for a moment, trying to fathom the most important thing...the one thing he hadn't spelt out.

'Are you saying that it would have happened with anyone...any girl who had come within arm's reach?' she asked him quietly, knowing that if he said yes it would break her heart.

When Diego avoided her eyes, frowning and looking impatient, the relief was acute.

He said, with a sarcastic snap, 'I'm not yet at the stage to make indiscriminate grabs at any woman who comes near me. I don't think you realise how very attractive you are...how unconsciously seductive.' His voice changed, becoming gentler. 'You're young for your age,

Lucinda. You've been out of the world for two years. You haven't been mixing with men...learning how to avoid inflammatory situations. A few months in Barcelona will change that. My parents will see that you meet people of your own age...young men to have light-hearted fun with.'

His expression didn't suggest that the prospect pleased him, she thought, hope reanimating.

'But you're wrong,' she said, sweetly reasonable. 'I was out and about *before* I went into seclusion. From the age of seventeen to twenty I had quite a lot of boy-friends. I haven't missed out on the light-hearted fun stage, Diego. As for last night, if I'd wanted to repulse you I expect I could have managed it. You make yourself sound like some sort of ravening satyr, but the fact is we were both enjoying it until you suddenly had an attack of scruples.'

This time it was he who flushed, dark colour spreading across the slant of his cheekbones under the olive skin which during their time in Tortosa the sun had bur-nished to dark gold.

'Don't argue with me,' he said brusquely. 'My mind is made up. I'll see you at the weekend. Goodbye for the present.'

He was turning away, without shaking hands, when Lucinda said, 'There's something you've overlooked. If it weren't for Oliver Thornham bringing pressure to bear, you wouldn't have brought me to Spain. What is he going to think about this change of plan?'

'I don't give a damn what he thinks. I am not his lackey,' he said, even more curtly.

'Also Laurian is expecting me to help her organise a Christmas house-party at the *parador*.'

'You can do that by telephone. You can come down with them at Christmas—I have no objections to that. Until then you're staying here. Is that understood?'

Without waiting for her reply he strode across the marble floor and disappeared into the house.

Lucinda spent all the next day with her father.

There had been little opportunity to talk privately the previous night when, during dinner and afterwards, he had won the *marqueses'* approbation with his agreeable manners and amusing traveller's tales. She knew now that one of her parents was entirely acceptable to them— even though the connection wasn't a legal one.

But the secret of her mother's identity still weighed on her, and more heavily than Diego's refusal to let her go south with him. In fact, now she had had time to think over their stormy parting, it no longer troubled her.

In light of careful thought, his behaviour now seemed very much what one might expect of a man of his age and background when he found himself powerfully attracted to a much younger woman who he guessed, correctly, had had no other lovers.

I don't think you realise how very attractive you are...how unconsciously seductive. He had as good as admitted that he wanted her, and with someone like Diego passion would be inextricably bound up with mental rapport. If it were not so, he wouldn't have deprived himself of physical love for so long.

And when I go down at Christmas, he'll find out how *consciously* seductive I can be, Lucinda had thought to herself, after waking this morning and lying in bed daydreaming of how it would be to wake up in Diego's arms after a long night of love.

Although not as perfect as being taken about by Diego, exploring Barcelona with her father was very enjoyable.

He insisted on taking her shopping—'I have twenty-two birthdays and Christmases to catch up on'—and Lucinda herself didn't want to leave finding presents for Diego and Rosa until the last moment. But she wouldn't allow Roderick to shower her with all the things he wanted to buy for her.

'Have you a fur coat?' he asked. 'It can be cold here after Christmas. They had snow a couple of years ago.'

'Yes, but it was most unusual, and I'm not a fur coat person. Even fur farms bother me, and I couldn't wear the fur of an animal which had been trapped.'

Next to the expensive furrier was a branch of Loewe, Spain's most famous leather specialists. He tried to persuade her to try on a coat in the window.

Lucinda laughed and shook her head. 'Do you know what I should like?'

'Tell me.'

'One hundred scarlet candles. They aren't really red, but they look it when they're alight.'

'What on earth do you want a hundred candles for?' he asked curiously.

'To take to Pobla de Cabres to light the church on Christmas Eve. I'm going to organise a crèche and carol-singing. I want it to be the most magical Christmas Rosa has ever had.'

'You really love that child, don't you?'

'Yes, I do. Well, you've met her...don't you think she's a poppet?'

Roderick nodded. 'Is it possible you're a little bit in love with her father?'

For a moment Lucinda hesitated to reveal her feelings about Diego even to him. Then she said, 'Not just a little bit. I'm head-over-heels mad about him. Why do you look like that? Don't *you* like him...what you've seen of him?'

'I liked the *look* of him—yes. I think it's a pity he's older than you and a widower.'

'He's only ten years older, which is about right, *I* think. As for his being a widower...I should like to have been his first and only love, but I'd settle for being his last and longest love. I'm not *sure* he loves me at all...I just think he *might*...I hope so.'

Over lunch she confided her anxiety about the Montfalcós' reactions when they found out about Georgia. The truth about Diego's marriage was not something she would pass on to anyone, not even her father, but she made it clear that the family was more than ordinarily anti-feminist.

'Is your mother really so famous now?' asked Roderick. 'I never see the sort of periodicals which would be likely to publicise her activities. I'm out of touch with half the goings on in the world, for that matter. When one spends most of one's life in out-of-the-way places, the political crises and other upheavals which loom large in most people's minds come to seem passing storms of no lasting importance.'

'Georgia is famous,' she assured him. 'She's rather like a volcano. Nothing much happens for a while and then she erupts and attracts a lot of publicity.'

'I don't see how you can be held responsible for her carryings on, particularly as you were brought up by your grandparents. If Diego is in love with you, he won't be put off by your mother. Nevertheless I should keep her under wraps until you know where you stand with him. It's not as if she were a murderess or a madwoman—at least not in the clinical sense. These bees in her bonnet about equality...who's to say she's not right? Had we been married, she would either have had to come on my expeditions or be left behind for long periods. She's probably enjoyed her life more doing her thing rather than mine.'

'She could also have had you *and* her career. That doesn't seem to have occurred to her,' said Lucinda. 'I can't see why one can't be a wife and a feminist. The two states don't have to be contradictory.' She flashed a smile at the waiter as he refilled her wine glass. 'If I write to tell her about the book, shall I mention meeting you? Or would you rather I didn't?'

Her father shrugged. 'That's up to you. I don't mind either way.'

It was impossible to tell if he still had some feelings for Georgia...a lingering tenderness which had survived the years since their love affair. Probably not, Lucinda decided. Having sought Georgia out once, after their quarrel, he hadn't made a second attempt to heal the breach between them.

The *marqueses* had arranged to spend Christmas in Madrid with their elder son and his wife. They would be returning to Barcelona for the New Year's Eve celebrations, and the whole family, including Mateo's and their daughters' parents-in-law, would assemble at the Casa Montfalcó for Los Reyes on January the sixth. This was when the main present-giving took place, and all over Spain the Three Kings, the Magi, came riding through the streets of cities, towns and the larger villages.

Bon Nadal—Christmas Day—was still mainly a religious festival, although commercial pressures were bringing it into line with the orgies of shopping and cooking which went on in other countries. Lucinda wanted to give Rosa the things which had made Christmas magical for her as a child: the shining tree, the stocking at the foot of the bed on Christmas morning, the crib with the carved wooden figures bought long ago at a Christmas market in Germany.

'Why aren't you at Pobla de Cabres?' asked Laurian Thornham, when Lucinda had to tell her that she would be liaising with the management of the *parador* from Barcelona.

'It's actually easier to organise things from here and more fun for Rosa. We'll be going to the village early in the New Year,' Lucinda answered, hoping this reckless statement would turn out to be true.

Diego rang up every night to have a chat with his child, but he didn't ask to speak to Lucinda. However, when he came home at the weekend his manner was friendly and relaxed. Although he could easily have chosen to spend time alone with Rosa, he seemed to want Lucinda to join them in all their activities.

'Is your father still here?' he asked her when, on Saturday afternoon, they were viewing the city from the heights of Montjuich.

'No, he's gone to London for a meeting at the Royal Geographic Society. But he'd like to join us at Tortosa for Christmas, if you have no objection?'

'He'll be most welcome. It will be nice for you to have someone of your own there. I'm looking forward to meeting him. My father says he's an extremely interesting man. Do you usually hear from your mother at Christmas?'

Rosa was not within hearing. Thinking she might drop a hint that Georgia had some way-out views, Lucinda said, 'Mother's an atheist. She doesn't celebrate Christmas. I've written to tell her the news about the book which I thought would interest her. I may get a letter back some time in the New Year.'

She had sent her letter care of Georgia's publisher and given as her address the box number at the post office in Tortosa which was where mail for anyone living at Pobla de Cabres would have to be collected from until such time as the community there justified official deliveries.

That night the other members of the family came to dinner and had their *aperitivos* in the library. It was the first time Lucinda had been there since the night Diego had kissed her. She wondered if he had an equally vivid recollection of lying on the rug in the firelight.

When she ventured a glance in his direction, she was surprised to find him watching her with a faint smile on his lips. It faded when she caught his eye but, instead of turning away, he continued to look at her until one of the children claimed his attention. She was left with the feeling that whatever he had been thinking when she caught him watching her, it had been something pleasant, something she would have liked if only she could have read his mind.

On Christmas Eve, as darkness fell on the village of Pobla de Cabres, one by one the wicks of a hundred candles in ruby-red containers took light from Lucinda's taper and gradually shed a bright, gently flickering glow over the bare interior of the church and the *plaza* outside it. Soon afterwards the first verse of 'Once In Royal David's City' rang out over the rooftops, followed by other popular carols sung with cheerful gusto by Oliver Thornham and his guests.

They had been at Pobla de Cabres since early afternoon when, following a picnic lunch, Oliver had shown his friends round and explained his vision of what the village would be like when the restoration was complete.

Later, after glasses of wine which had been mulled in the kitchen of Diego's house-cum-office had been handed round, with pieces of *turrón*, a traditional Spanish sweetmeat, the majority of the party piled into a hired mini-bus for the drive back to Tortosa. Led by Diego and Rosa in the Land Rover, with Oliver driving the bus and Roderick at the wheel of the BMW in the rear, the three-vehicle convoy set off down the still-rutted road.

Two hours later, leaving Rosa tucked up in bed and already soundly asleep after an exciting day, Lucinda went to join the others in the bar. Tonight she wasn't wearing one of her mother's discards but a new outfit which Laurian had brought for her: a cat-suit of silvery-grey crushed velvet, as strokable as pussy-willow catkins, with a wide belt of soft matching leather which emphasised her small waist.

Diego had come to kiss Rosa good night while Lucinda was still in her bathrobe, starting to put on the new eye make-up she had seen demonstrated in the cosmetics department of El Corte Inglés, a department store in Barcelona. Recognising his knock on the door, she had whisked into the bathroom so that he shouldn't see her before the effect was complete.

Most of the others were in the bar before her, a cosmopolitan group including two American couples, a Frenchman, an Italian girl, and four English couples, Laurian's original guest list having expanded as Christmas approached. They were all what she called achievers, meaning interesting people leading hardworking, fulfilled lives. At one time Lucinda might have felt slightly intimidated by them. Now, in the light of John Sidmouth's encouraging words about her verses and the extracts from her diary, she felt she had the potential to become an achiever herself.

The moment she entered the bar, Diego detached himself from the others and came towards her, as if he had been waiting for her.

'You're like a chameleon,' he said, with a sweeping appraisal which took in her upswept hair, the close-fitting velvet cat-suit, its silver zipper open to form a deep V showing rather more cleavage than she usually exposed. 'At the barbecue, with a *bocadillo* in one hand and a bottle of Coke in the other, you looked about ten years older than Rosa. Tonight you're glamour personified.'

'Thank you.'

Spoken in another tone, his comment could have been teasing. But the look in his eyes wasn't amused. Instinct told her that he was remembering the night when his lips had caressed the soft flesh laid bare by the open teeth of the zipper. She knew, had they been alone, he would have been tempted to pull her into his arms.

'I've made a slight alteration to the table plan which you and Laurian worked out,' he told her. 'I've put myself on one side of you. I hope you don't object.'

'I'm flattered.'

'Come and have something to drink.'

As she moved towards the bar, he came closer, his arm going behind her back, his hand falling lightly on her shoulder in a gesture which had, she thought—hoped!—something definitely proprietorial about it.

She was taking her first sip of champagne, and thinking how dashing he looked in the dinner jacket which Laurian had asked all the men to wear tonight, when Oliver came up to them.

'You look a knock-out, Lucinda. Is Rosa asleep or too excited about her nocturnal visitor?'

'Fast asleep. But I have a strong suspicion that I'm going to be awake a lot earlier than the rest of you tomorrow morning,' she said, with a laugh.

'Listen, I've had an idea,' he said. 'Diego has told me about your grandfather's book and your part in it. How about starting a Pobla de Cabres diary? A record of all that goes on during the restoration with character sketches of the people involved. Suitably illustrated, it could make an interesting story, and——' He broke off, the lift of his eyebrows indicating surprise at something happening by the door.

Although a number of townspeople had booked to dine at the *parador* later tonight, no other people were staying there apart from the Thornham's party.

So it was somebody Spanish whom Lucinda expected to see when she looked round.

But the woman who had just entered, and whose striking appearance was already causing a hiatus in the conversation of everyone already present, wasn't Spanish, although her first words, addressed to the company in general, were, *'Buenas noches.'*

She strolled further into the room, the slit in the skirt of her long dress giving a glimpse of good legs in sheer black tights, her neckline making Lucinda's seem modest by comparison.

'Good evening,' said Georgia Garforth. 'Is this a private party, or can a benighted traveller join in?'

There was a hush, lasting two or three seconds, before Laurian moved forward, half welcoming, half astonished.

'Georgia! What in the world are you doing here? Are you alone?'

'Not now...I was a minute ago. What a welcome sight *you* are.' Georgia embraced her with enthusiasm. She drew back. 'I had visions of a solitary supper and an early night...not very festive.'

'But why are you here in Tortosa?'

'You may well ask! This morning I was in Andorra where a friend of mine has a ski lodge. Take my advice: never go there. The sun hasn't shone for three days. I didn't even *glimpse* the mountains; they were hidden behind thick grey clouds. And not only did it pour with rain all the time I was there, but the other guests were a dull lot...'

She paused to glance briefly at the rest of her listeners, but failed to notice Lucinda among them, her eyes wide with shock and dismay.

'...not like your jolly-looking group,' Georgia continued. 'So this morning I got a lift to Barcelona and there I rented a car and drove myself here. One of my many mad impulses!'

'Why here?' asked Laurian.

'Because I know someone in this area. But unfortunately the only address I have is a box number, and the post office was closed by the time I found it and won't reopen until after Christmas. So there was nothing for it but to find an hotel and make the best of things.'

'What a godsend for you that we're here,' said Laurian. 'Let me introduce you.' She turned to her guests. 'This is Georgia Garforth, one of my most famous customers. Most of you will know her by sight and reputation. Georgia, this is Ludovic Thierry from Paris...'

'*Enchanté, madame.*'

'...Peter and Patty Rochester from New York...'

'Glad to know you, Georgia.'

'...and Roderick Tresillian who——'

But whatever Laurian had intended to say about him was cut off by Georgia's gasped, 'Oh, my God!' and her visible consternation.

'Georgia and I have met before,' Roderick said quietly. Then, with sharp urgency, 'Look out, she's going to——'

As Georgia swayed, he sprang forward to save her from falling. With the presence of mind of a man accustomed to emergencies, he supported her to the nearest chair, where he bent her forward until her head was hanging over her knees.

Exclamations of concern had eddied among the onlookers. Someone behind Lucinda murmured, 'Fancy a feminist fainting! Seems out of character...'

The comment, perhaps not meant unkindly, lit a spurt of anger in her. To be faced, at the end of a long and fruitless journey, with the father of one's child, not seen for more than twenty years, was enough to make anyone keel over. Her own feelings swept aside by her concern for her mother, Lucinda hurried across to her parents.

'Let's get her up to her room. We can't sort this out in public,' she muttered to Roderick.

'You're right.' He turned to Laurian, who was hovering anxiously at his elbow. 'Sorry about this. Don't hold back dinner for us. It may be better for Georgia to have something on a tray upstairs.'

She nodded, her lovely face concerned and puzzled.

With an ease which surprised everyone else but not Lucinda, who had seen him stripped to the waist and knew what powerful muscles were concealed by a dinner jacket which had probably been made for him the better part of thirty years ago, Roderick picked Georgia up and, with Oliver holding open the door and Lucinda at his heels, carried her out of the bar.

By the time one of the staff sprang forward to open another door for them, Georgia was reviving and demanding to be put down.

When he ignored her, she said, 'You'll give yourself a heart attack. I'm not a piece of thistledown, and you're too old for these macho displays.'

'Yes, you have put on weight, haven't you?'

'Not one pound,' she informed him icily. 'My weight is exactly the same as the last time you showed off like this.'

'Your tongue is as sharp as ever too. Fortunately our daughter hasn't inherited your waspishness. I was pleasantly surprised to find her so sweet-tempered and feminine. Your mother's influence, no doubt.'

'Our daughter?' echoed Georgia, in a very different tone.

'Lucinda. She's right behind us.'

Georgia peered over his shoulder. '*Lucinda*...My God! Have I gone mad? When did you—— How long have you two known each other?'

'Long enough to find out that you did us both a major disservice by keeping us apart,' Roderick said curtly. 'We'll discuss that later. For the time being, kindly be quiet.'

With a meekness which would have astonished the readers of *The Better Half*, she obeyed him.

Lucinda was carrying the quilted black satin evening bag, recognisably Chanel, which had slipped from her mother's shoulder while she slumped in the chair. It contained the key to her room.

Having set Georgia on her feet by the bed and told her to lie down, Roderick picked up the telephone and asked room service to bring coffee for three. He then gave Lucinda his key and asked her to fetch a bottle of brandy from his wardrobe.

When she returned from this errand, he said to her, 'I think you should rejoin the others. Georgia and I may reappear or we may not. We have a lot to talk about.'

Lucinda looked at her mother, who now had her shoes off and three pillows stacked behind her.

'Yes, don't let my sudden appearance wreck your evening,' said Georgia. 'After making an idiot of myself,

I need time to recover my poise. I'll be back on form in the morning. I'm glad I've found you. Off you go, darling.'

Roderick put his arm round Lucinda and steered her towards the door. 'Diego is very astute. By now he'll have put two and two together... sized up the situation. You won't have to explain it. Don't worry, it will be all right. He's a very sound chap in my judgement. Enjoy yourself. Happy Christmas!'

He brushed a kiss on her temple, opened the door and pushed her gently into the corridor.

At the end of the corridor, where it opened out to form a landing, Diego was standing. He had his hands in his pockets and looked as if he might have been pacing back and forth but had checked when he heard the door open.

Lucinda walked slowly towards him, wondering if he *had* grasped the truth and, if he had, whether it would be all right, as Roderick has assured her.

When she came near, Diego asked, 'Is she better now?'

'A bit limp still. Roderick will look after her. She's my mother... or had you gathered that?'

He nodded, taking his hands from his pockets. 'It all fitted together... her coming here... being knocked sideways at meeting him. You're not at all like her.'

'No... not in the least.'

He held out his hands, palms upwards. After a little hesitation, not quite sure if the gesture was merely an offer of comfort after the shock she herself had experienced, Lucinda put her hands into his.

His fingers closed firmly round hers. 'I was wondering, while I was waiting, if we might give them another surprise later on.'

'What kind of surprise?'

'I should like to tell them that you and I are going to be married...or am I taking entirely too much for granted?'

When she didn't answer, being speechless with joy, he went on, 'I've wanted to say "I love you" for some time, but I forced myself not to because...well, mainly because you're so young. You should have more time to explore all the options.'

'Oh, Diego—once you love someone there *are* no options. Don't you know that? Everything else in life has to be fitted around the one most important thing of all...sharing your life with the person you love.'

She pulled her hands free, but only in order to fling her arms round his neck.

'What's the use of fame or success or money if, like my mother, on Christmas Eve you have to drive hundreds of miles in search of a daughter you hardly ever see and didn't intend to visit in the first place? It's just chance that she's not alone here with no one but the barman and the waiters to talk to. At her age that's sad...pathetic. You and Rosa are my priorities. All the other options are secondary.'

She felt his arms tighten, then slacken again. 'I didn't mean only those possibilities. There are hundreds of men in the world who could make you happy. Have I the right to tie you down when you ought, by all sensible standards, to wait till your middle twenties or later. I'm mature, I'm not going to change. You're still a half-open bud. It can be a terrible mistake for people to marry too young.'

'Yes, I know...as it was for you and Rosa's mother—your mother told me about it. But maturity isn't only a matter of age. It's like wisdom. Some people are never wise, even when they're old, and some are never mature.

Darling Diego, I'm not only *in* love with you, in a young way... I love you... in a lasting way.'

At this he hugged her so tightly that she gasped, and her parted lips made him forget all his misgivings and apply himself to kissing her.

Very early the following morning Lucinda was woken by Rosa, who had not only discovered her own Christmas stocking but had noticed there was another at the foot of Lucinda's bed.

Together—in Lucinda's case with somewhat modified enthusiasm as it wasn't yet seven and she hadn't got to bed until one—they opened the surprises prepared for them. Lucinda had helped Diego to fill the child's stocking with little fun things. The contents of her own stocking included such things as jazzy micro-briefs from Marks & Spencer which must have been brought back from London by her father, and also one very lavish gift which she knew must be a gift from her future husband.

This was a leather case, the satin lining stamped with the name of a leading Barcelona jeweller, containing a beautiful pair of Art Nouveau ear-rings set with opals and pearls and obviously chosen to complement her pendant.

When, later, she thanked Diego for them, he said, 'The jeweller is reserving for me a ring made at the same period which I think you might like for your engagement ring. To bring it with me seemed altogether too presumptuous.'

'I don't know why... since my feelings must have been obvious to you after that night in the library,' said Lucinda.

'Mm... your behaviour did seem to indicate a certain partiality.' He pulled her close. 'Thinking about that night makes it hard for me to be patient. What a fool I was not to make sure you had your own bedroom this time!'

She shared his impatience, but knew there would be very little chance of their snatching more than a short time alone together while they were part of the *parador* party. She also knew he wouldn't make serious love to her until they could be sure of uninterrupted privacy in a perfect setting for the first rapturous fusion of their eager bodies.

After breakfast they telephoned his brother's number in Madrid to break their news to his parents.

When the Marqués spoke to Lucinda, he said, 'The first time I met Julia I knew she would be my wife. It was the same when I saw you. My instinct told me, "This girl is right for Diego." I'm delighted to hear my instinct was once again right and I'm sure you'll both be as happy as we've been. We'll look forward to seeing you on New Year's Eve, my dear.'

The next people to be told were the Thornhams, who were also delighted. Later, Laurian confided that it was she who had persuaded her husband to use his influence with Diego to secure the job in Spain for Lucinda.

'I was certain, right from the outset, that you were the ideal girl for him. Oliver didn't want to interfere, but I coaxed him,' she said, pleased with the successful outcome of her machination.

About half the Thornhams' guests had had breakfast in bed or on their sunny balconies, and it was not until noon that everyone gathered to set out for another picnic, this time on the long, empty beach on the seaward edge of the delta.

As she had said she would be, Georgia was back on form, charming the women as well as the men, and behaving as if she had never concealed from anyone that she had a grown-up daughter.

Whether she and Roderick felt an obligation, as guests, to assume an air of affability towards each other, or whether they had really reached a degree of amity, was impossible to tell.

'What do you think?' Lucinda asked Diego, as they walked by the water's edge, not out of sight of the others but out of earshot.

'Last night, after we'd said good night, I tried to imagine how I should feel if I'd missed knowing my child,' he said. 'A deception as serious as that can't be easy to forgive. Are you hoping they'll get together? I shouldn't count on it, my love.'

'I don't,' she assured him. 'For a time, after Grandfather died, I did feel rather bereft. But now, all at once, I seem to have all the family and friends anyone could wish for. You and Rosa...Roderick...your parents...the Thornhams...'

Diego looked along the beach to where Roderick was helping to light the portable barbecues while Georgia was chatting to Patty Rochester.

'On the other hand,' he said thoughtfully, 'they're two lonely people who had something going for them once. Perhaps this time they'll make it work.'

'Perhaps,' Lucinda agreed.

Their clasped hands exchanged a firmer pressure. They smiled into each other's eyes. There was no perhaps about their shared future.

Harlequin Presents

Coming Next Month

Harlequin Historicals

Step into a world of pulsing adventure, gripping emotion and lush sensuality with these evocative love stories penned by today's best-selling authors in the highest romantic tradition. Pursuing their passionate dreams against a backdrop of the past's most colorful and dramatic moments, our vibrant heroines and dashing heroes will make history come alive for you.

Watch for two new Harlequin Historicals each month, available wherever Harlequin books are sold. History was never so much fun—you won't want to miss a single moment!